"Let Me Be The Big Strong Man. Let Me Be Your Man,"

Frank said, grabbing Leenie by the shoulders.

"You want to be a buffer between me and the big bad world, don't you?"

"Something like that," he replied. "After all, I am Andrew's father. I wasn't around while you were pregnant or when you gave birth. I should have been. I need to be the one to bring Andrew home safe to you. I need to do this for you."

Leenie swallowed, then offered him a fragile smile, before he cupped her face with his hands then kissed her.

* * *

"Beverly Barton writes with searing emotional intensity that tugs at every heartstring."
—*New York Times* **bestselling author Linda Howard**

Dear Reader,

Welcome back to another passionate month at Silhouette Desire. *A Scandal Between the Sheets* is breaking out as Brenda Jackson pens the next tale in the scintillating DYNASTIES: THE DANFORTHS series. We all love the melodrama and mayhem that surrounds this Southern family—how about you?

The superb Beverly Barton stops by Silhouette Desire with an extra wonderful title in her bestselling series THE PROTECTORS. *Keeping Baby Secret* will keep *you* on the edge of your seat—and curl your toes all at the same time. What would you do if you had to change your name and your entire history? Sheri WhiteFeather tackles that compelling question when her heroine is forced to enter the witness protection program in *A Kept Woman*. Seems she was a kept woman of another sort, as well…so be sure to pick up this fabulous read if you want the juicy details.

Kristi Gold has written the final, fabulous installment of THE TEXAS CATTLEMAN'S CLUB: THE STOLEN BABY series with *Fit for a Sheikh*. (But don't worry, we promise those sexy cattlemen with be back.) And rounding out the month are two wonderful stories filled with an extra dose of passion: Linda Conrad's dramatic *Slow Dancing With A Texan* and Emilie Rose's supercharged *A Passionate Proposal*.

Enjoy all we have to offer this month—and every month—at Silhouette Desire.

Melissa Jeglinski

Melissa Jeglinski
Senior Editor, Silhouette Desire

Please address questions and book requests to:
Silhouette Reader Service
U.S.: 3010 Walden Ave., P.O. Box 1325, Buffalo, NY 14269
Canadian: P.O. Box 609, Fort Erie, Ont. L2A 5X3

B E V E R L Y
BARTON

Keeping baby secret

Published by Silhouette Books

America's Publisher of Contemporary Romance

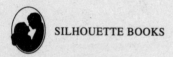 **SILHOUETTE BOOKS**

ISBN 0-373-76574-6

KEEPING BABY SECRET

Copyright © 2004 by Beverly Beaver

Printed in U.S.A.

Books by Beverly Barton

BEVERLY BARTON

has been in love with romance since her grandfather gave her an illustrated book of *Beauty and the Beast*. An avid reader since childhood, Beverly wrote her first book at nine. After marriage to her own "hero" and the births of her daughter and son, Beverly chose to be a full-time homemaker, aka wife, mother, friend and volunteer. This author of over thirty-five books is a member of Romance Writers of America and helped found the Heart of Dixie chapter. She has won numerous awards, and has made the Waldenbooks and *USA TODAY* bestseller lists.

In loving memory of our cocker spaniel, Cole,
who was my faithful companion for nearly fifteen years.

Prologue

Leenie checked the refrigerator for the third time. The bottles of milk were there, as she knew they would be. Just where she'd put them. But she simply had to check a final time, had to make sure nothing had been left undone. After all, this was a turning point in her life, a make-or-break night. As she hurried by the computer desk in her kitchen, she glanced at the list of phone numbers posted by the telephone. Emergency numbers, her cell number, her private number at work, as well as the switchboard number.

Rushing out of the kitchen and down the hall, her heartbeat rapid and her stomach painfully knotted, she wondered why this had to be so difficult. It wasn't as if she was the first woman in the world to go through this painful separation. Millions of women throughout the world had done what she was doing and most of them could probably sympathize with her feelings of guilt and fear.

As she neared the end of the hall, she slowed her pace, took a deep breath and told herself that she could do this. She was a strong woman. An independent woman. When she reached the nursery, she looked from Debra, who smiled compassionately, to Andrew, who lay sleeping peacefully in his bed, totally unaware of the trauma his mother was experiencing.

"Everything will be all right." Debra draped her arm around Leenie's shoulders. "You'll be gone only a few hours and he'll probably sleep the entire time you're away."

"But if he wakes and I'm not here..." Leenie pulled away from her son's nanny, walked over to Andrew's bassinet and watched her six-week-old baby as he slept. His little chest rose and fell softly with each tender breath he took. She reached out to touch his rosy cheek.

"If he wakes, I'll be right here," Debra assured her. "And if he's hungry, you left breast milk in the fridge. You aren't deserting him forever, you're just going to work."

"Maybe we should postpone this another week or so." Leenie couldn't bear the thought of being separated from Andrew, even for the four hours it would take her to drive to WJMM, do her two-hour midnight talk-show on the radio, set things up for her morning TV show and then drive home.

"No, we won't postpone it," Debra said firmly. "We can continue taking Andrew to the station every morning for your daytime show, but he shouldn't be dragged out of his bed every night." Debra crossed her arms over her chest and narrowed her gaze. "Go to work, Leenie. You do your job and let me do mine."

Sighing heavily, Leenie admitted her deepest fears. "But one of my jobs is being Andrew's mother and if you do your job too well, my son will bond with you and not me."

Huffing loudly, but following up with an understanding smile, Debra patted Leenie's arm. "Andrew has already bonded with you. He knows you're his mother. If I do my job well, and I'd like to think I've been doing that since the day we brought Andrew home from the hospital, then he'll think of me as a favorite aunt or as a grandmother."

"I'm being silly, aren't I?"

"No, you're being a good mother."

"Am I a good mother? I'm not sure what makes a good mother. As you well know, I didn't have one of my own. No mother at all raised me, good, bad or otherwise."

"Jerry and I were parents to over fifty foster kids in our thirty years of marriage." Debra sighed dreamily, as she always did whenever she mentioned her late husband, who had died two years ago at the age of sixty-three from a heart attack. "I've seen all kinds of mothers and I know a good one from a bad one."

"Yes, I imagine you do. You were certainly an excellent role model for me when I lived with you and Jerry. I learned by watching the way you were with all of us foster children what a good mother is." She had been fifteen when she'd been sent to live with Debra and Jerry Schmale, a young minister and his wife who'd been told they could never have children of their own and had decided they would give their love and time to unwanted, neglected kids of all ages. The three years she'd spent with the Schmales had been the best years of her childhood.

"You, Dr. Lurleen Patton, are a good mother," Debra said.

"Even though I'm a single parent? Even though I didn't provide Andrew with a father?"

"You told me that Andrew was the result of a very brief affair with a man you barely knew. A man who showed no interest in settling down. A man who was very careful to use protection each time y'all made love."

Leenie nodded. "One of those times, that protection failed. Otherwise, I wouldn't have gotten pregnant. But that wasn't Frank's fault."

"You made the decision not to tell Andrew's father about his existence because you felt it was the best thing for everyone concerned. Right?"

"Right."

"Have you changed your mind?"

No, she hadn't changed her mind. Although, truth be told, sometimes she wished she had called Frank the day she'd found out she was pregnant, called him and told him he was going to be a daddy. But she'd been so shocked herself that it had taken her weeks to figure out what to do. By the time she decided she wanted to keep her baby and raise it herself, she had also decided that the last thing Frank Latimer would want in his life was a child. Their entire relationship had lasted less than two weeks. Love hadn't been involved. Just a major case of lust.

"No, I haven't changed my mind. If Frank knew he had a child, it would simply complicate his life and mine, not to mention Andrew's."

Debra turned Leenie around, grasped her shoulders and all but shoved her out of the room. "If you don't leave now, you'll be late." Debra walked Leenie into the hallway and all the way to the back door. "Call me every thirty minutes, if that will make you feel better—but go. Now!"

Leenie sighed. "Thanks. I don't know what I'd do without you. Sometimes I think I need you even more than Andrew does."

Debra hugged her, then lifted Leenie's jacket and purse from where they hung on a coatrack near the door, handed them to her and said, "Drive carefully, call as often as you need to, have a great show tonight and I'll be waiting up for you when you come home."

Leenie slipped into her coat, draped her purse straps over her shoulder and opened the back door that led into the garage. She unlocked her new GMC Envoy SUV, a vehicle she'd purchased a month before her son's birth. Of course she'd kept her sports car, but hadn't used it since Andrew had been born because she never went anywhere without him. Use it tonight, she told herself. Get in your Mustang and fly off down the road.

After locking the SUV, she went over to the Mustang, unlocked it and got in, then revved the motor and hit the remote that opened the garage. Within minutes she was zipping along the highway that led from the suburbs of Maysville, Mississippi, into the downtown area where the studios for both WJMM radio and TV stations were located. She'd been doing a late-night radio talk show and a morning TV show for quite a few years and enjoyed being a local celebrity, a psychiatrist who doled out advice over the airwaves five days and nights a week.

When she'd been younger, she had longed to create a family of her own. Having grown up in a series of foster homes and remembering very little about her own parents, she had always felt so alone. Her mother had died when she was four and her father when she was eight. A skinny, gangly girl, who had talked too much and tried too hard to make others like her, she'd never had a real chance of being adopted. From eight to eighteen, she'd been shifted around from foster home to foster home. She'd felt unloved and unwanted all her life and by the time she hit thirty and Prince Charming hadn't entered her life, she'd pretty much given up hope for that fantasized happily ever after ending in her life.

Although she'd been around the block a few times, as the old saying went, she wasn't promiscuous. Each time she'd been in a committed relationship, she'd wanted it to be "the one." And she'd never had a one-night stand. Not until Frank Latimer entered her life. Or should she say breezed in and out of her life. And technically, he hadn't really been a one-night stand. More like a ten day mini-affair. She'd taken one look at the big lug and fallen hard and fast. They had set the sheets on fire and what she'd thought would be a one-nighter turned into a very brief, extremely passionate relationship.

Leenie wished it wasn't late November already so she could put the top down on her car and achieve that wild and free feeling it gave her to ride with the wind. Maybe that's what she needed—some cold night air to clear away the cobwebs. As hard as she tried to relegate Frank Latimer to the back of her mind, to put him into the past where he belonged, she found it difficult, if not impossible, to do. Although

Andrew had her blond hair and blue eyes, he resembled Frank or the way she was sure Frank had looked as a baby. And every time she looked at her son, she saw his father. How could she—a psychiatrist who'd been trained to understand the human psyche—have ever thought she'd be able to forget about the man who had fathered her child? Whether or not he was actually in her life, he'd always be a part of it. Andrew was the living, breathing proof of that.

She'd told Debra that she wasn't having any second thoughts about contacting Frank to let him know he had a child, but maybe she'd been lying to herself as well as Debra. Maybe she should call Frank, feel him out, see if there was somebody special in his life these days. Or maybe she should just fly to Atlanta and take Andrew with her. No, she couldn't do that, couldn't just show up on Frank's doorstep.

Stop debating the issue, she told herself. *You're not going to call Frank.* And she wasn't going to fly to Atlanta. If he had the slightest interest in renewing his relationship with her, he'd have called by now. After all, it was over ten months since he'd said goodbye and walked out of her life without a backward glance. She had to accept the fact that Frank wasn't her Prince Charming, accept the fact that there was no such animal. Just because he'd been different from the other men she'd known didn't mean she was as special to him as he had been to her. What they'd had wasn't love. It was just sex.

One

Leenie glanced across the table at Jim Isbell, a good-looking, likable guy. He had asked her out after their initial meeting last week when he'd appeared on her morning TV show in a segment about group therapy. Jim was a psychologist who worked with families in trouble—drugs, alcohol, infidelity and various other problems that plagued many people in today's complex modern society. This was their first date—one she'd been looking forward to eagerly. It was a simple workday lunch between friends. No strings attached. Nothing that would put pressure on either of them. Everyone who knew her, including Debra, had encouraged her to start dating again. After all, she hadn't been out with a man since she'd found out she was pregnant. Now Andrew was nearly two months old and adjusting beautifully to having a working mother. Debra brought him to the studio several days a week, but kept him home in his own bed at night. Although Leenie loved her job, her son was the center of her world.

"So, are you interested?" Jim asked.

"Hmm?"

"Dinner and a movie this weekend," Jim said.

"Oh, uh…yes. That might be nice." Nice. Such an odd word, with so many meanings. And often a bland word, one that conveyed very little emotion. *Oh, jeez, Leenie, don't overanalyze your response about the date. You meant the word nice in the…well, in the nicest way.* She smiled to herself. *You like Jim. Obviously he likes you. You've had a pleasant lunch, so why not follow up with a dinner date?*

Nice? Pleasant? Why not fantastic or great or fabulous or wonderful? What if Frank Latimer asked her out for a dinner date? *You wouldn't be using such lukewarm adjectives, now would you?* An inner voice taunted. *Stop it!* She shouldn't compare Jim to Frank. They were apples and oranges. Yeah, sure they were, but Jim was such a boring apple and Frank had been such an incredible orange.

Frank with the sexy gray eyes and hard, lean body. Frank, who had memorized every inch of her with his bedroom eyes, with his big hands and his mouth and tongue. Frank, who always looked like an unmade bed and had a way of curling her toes without even touching her.

"Lurleen?"

"Huh?" Apparently Jim had said something to which he expected a response and since she'd been thinking about another man, she hadn't heard a word Jim had said.

"You're a million miles away, aren't you?"

"Sorry, Jim, it's just that I—"

"No need to explain. You're thinking about your son, aren't you? New mothers tend to obsess about their babies. But you really should work your way through those typical feelings about neglecting and abandoning your child in favor of your career. You're too smart to believe that you have to be the most important person in his life right now. After all, you have a perfectly capable nanny, don't you?"

"Yes, a very capable nanny."

"I understand that you have an extra burden of guilt on your shoulders since you're a single mother."

Leenie stared at Jim as he continued talking, giving her his opinion about the correct way to rear children, especially a son without a father figure. Not one to take criticism or advice well, his comments aggravated her. Who was he to be giving her advice? Had she asked him to share his wisdom on the subject of raising children?

"Jim!"

With his mouth open midsentence, he stopped talking and looked quizzically at her. "Yes?"

She'd been about to lambaste him, tell him in no uncertain terms that her relationship with her son was none of his damn business. Instead she said, "Let's order dessert. Cheesecake."

He arched his eyebrows in a disapproving manner. "Are you sure you want the extra calories? After all, you probably still have some baby fat you want to lose."

He smiled at her in his good-natured manner. And she wanted to slap him. Baby fat, indeed! She weighed now precisely what she'd weighed before she'd gotten pregnant, having dropped twenty pounds when Andrew was born and another ten in the past two months. Everyone else she knew had marveled over how quickly she'd gotten back in shape.

"Right. No dessert." It wasn't the calories she could do without, it was the company. She gritted her teeth to keep from telling him off in no uncertain terms. "Look, I just remembered that I have a previous engagement this weekend, so I'll have to forego dinner and a movie." She shoved back her chair and stood.

Ever the gentleman, Jim stood up. "Perhaps lunch again next week, then?"

"Perhaps." She picked up her purse.

"I'll call you."

"Please do. I hate to run, but—"

"Work awaits," he said.

"Yes."

She didn't bother to contradict him, to tell him she was going home where she'd spend the afternoon and early evening with Andrew. Nodding, she forced a smile, then hurried away from the table, out of the restaurant and to her car. Once inside, she checked her watch. Two-fifteen. She'd go on home and be there in time to help put away groceries. About now Debra and Andrew were at Foodland on their weekly shopping excursion. Usually Leenie joined them for lunch on Fridays and afterward they bought groceries together, but today she'd had a date. A waste of time. Time she could have spent with her son.

Wonder if it's too late to join them at Foodland? She could buy one of those frozen cheesecakes and indulge at supper tonight. That's what she'd do. Eat cheesecake and forget about Jim Isbell. Out there somewhere was another guy who wouldn't bore her to tears. Someone as much fun as Frank. As sexy as Frank. As good in bed as Frank.

All right already. Enough about Frank!

Frank is the past. Jim Isbell was a dud. Think about Andrew. And cheesecake.

Frank Latimer stretched out as best he could in his seat, thankful that he was in first class and not stuck back in coach. Most of the time when he flew, it was on the luxurious Dundee jet, but when his latest job had ended today, the jet was already en route to Key West, taking a crew of Dundee's best for a top secret assignment. He was set for a week off and planned to do some fishing while he relaxed at Sawyer Mc-Namara's Hilton Head vacation house. He'd been working practically nonstop for nearly a year now. When he'd left Maysville, Mississippi, eleven months ago, he'd taken a European assignment just to get him out of the country and as far away as was possible from a certain long and lean blonde. If there had been a flight to Mars eleven months ago, he'd have taken it.

"Would you care for another glass of tea, Mr. Latimer?" the attractive brunette flight attendant asked. He'd noticed her immediately, the minute he'd boarded his flight from Chicago to Atlanta. Ms. Gant was petite and slender, with big eyes and big boobs and a come-hither smile.

"No, thank you."

"Is there anything else I can do for you?"

Oh, yeah, there was something she could do for him all right. He was in bad need of a warm body in his bed. For months after his whirlwind affair with Leenie Patton, he hadn't touched another woman.

Then he'd convinced himself that what he needed to get Leenie out of his system was a woman—actually a lot of women. He'd tried that, but it hadn't worked. No one had tasted like Leenie or felt like Leenie or sounded like Leenie. So after gorging himself on nameless, faceless bed partners, he'd sworn off women altogether, at least until he could stop wanting one particular lady—a sexy, wild woman he'd called Slim.

"Mr. Latimer?"

"Huh?"

"Are you all right?"

"Yeah, sure. I'm fine."

No, he wasn't fine. He was tired. This last job had lasted six weeks and he'd been shot at twice and wound up in three fistfights. He badly needed some major down-time. And Sawyer's luxurious home in Hilton Head was just the ticket. If he could find a gorgeous, sexy blonde to spend the week with him, he'd have it made. It was time to end his months of celibacy.

The trouble is you don't want just any gorgeous, sexy blonde. You want Slim. She's what you want. All you want.

So why not call her up when he landed in Atlanta? And say what? *I've been thinking about you for eleven months? Every time I slept with somebody else, I wished she was you?*

"Hell, no!"

Frank didn't realize he'd cursed aloud until Ms. Gant said, "Yes, Mr. Latimer, did you say something?"

"Just talking to myself," he told her. "That happens when you get old."

She giggled like a teenager and flashed him a brilliant smile. "You're hardly old."

"I'm forty," he admitted, feeling every year of it.

"That's not old. That's the prime of life for a man."

He chuckled. "I thought prime time for a guy was eighteen."

She moistened her lips. "A man of forty has experience that a younger man doesn't. I prefer experience."

She's putting it out there for you, Latimer, he told himself. All you have to do is take what she's offering. He was tempted. Damn tempted. Even if she wasn't a long-legged, willowy blonde.

Leaning down close to his ear, she whispered, "I'll be in Atlanta overnight."

"How about dinner?" He'd definitely been celibate long enough. Months of doing without wasn't his style. It was time he tried sex again. And past time to get Leenie Patton out of his system.

Two blocks from Foodland, Leenie heard the wail of sirens—police and ambulance—and couldn't help wondering if there had been a bad wreck somewhere nearby. The first thought that flashed through her mind was that Andrew and Debra had been involved in the accident. But she quickly dismissed the idea as nothing more than her tendency to worry much too much about Andrew whenever he was out of her sight. Of course she understood that her worries, concerns and fears were perfectly natural, that almost every new mother experienced these emotions whether she was a working mom or a stay at home mom. Naturally, being a single parent only added to

her concerns about motherhood. With each passing
day of Andrew's life, Leenie felt more and more
guilty for not having contacted Frank to tell him about
their child. She had given herself every reason not to
call him, to keep Andrew's existence a secret from
him, but in the end she knew, in her heart of hearts,
that Frank had a right to know.

Admit it, she told herself, *you're scared to tell
Frank the truth.* If she told him and he didn't want
to be a part of Andrew's life, she'd wonder what kind
of man he really was. On the other hand, if he wanted
to be a part of his son's life, but didn't want her in
the bargain, then she'd have to not only share Andrew, but she'd have to accept the fact that she'd
never been special to Frank.

As she cruised down the tree-lined street at thirty-
five miles an hour, she forced her mind off Frank
Latimer and onto cheesecake. *Wonder if Foodland
has any chocolate cheesecake?* she mused.

Suddenly the Lexus in front of her eased to a halt
behind a line of other vehicles. Noting that the car's
brake lights had come on, Leenie stopped her SUV
and tried to see what lay ahead. Able to make out the
whirl of blue flashing lights in the distance, she figured traffic had been stopped at the scene of the accident about a block ahead of her. If the wreck had
just occurred, it could take quite a while to clear
things up and get traffic moving again. Her lane was
stalled and the other lane was empty, as if traffic had
been stopped on the other side of the police car up
ahead. She sighed. *I should have gone home instead
of heading to Foodland to meet up with Debra and
Andrew,* she thought. If she got stuck here for very

long, she'd call Debra on her cell phone to let her
know why she was delayed.

Tapping her fingers on the steering wheel, she
hummed. And waited. Suddenly an ambulance flew
by, its siren mournfully eerie. Once again, an odd
sensation hit Leenie in the pit of her stomach. Don't
do this to yourself, she cautioned. Stop thinking
Debra's Saturn was involved in the wreck. Debra and
Andrew were either still at Foodland or they were
stalled on the other side of the accident and were
waiting in line, just as she was.

As the minutes ticked by, Leenie tried to think of
other things. Her boring lunch date with Jim. The
topics she planned to discuss tonight on her midnight
radio show before she took phone calls. Andrew's
latest doctor's checkup when she'd been told he was
absolutely perfect, something she'd already known, of
course. Getting his two-month pictures made next
week. He was such a beautiful child. He had her col-
oring. Blond hair and blue eyes. But he had Frank's
mouth…and his little hands and feet were miniature
replicas of Frank's. Odd that she could remember so
well everything about a man she'd known for such a
brief time.

A heavyset guy in the truck ahead of the Lexus in
front of her got out and walked down the street, in
the direction of the wreck. It never ceased to amaze
her how curious people were about disasters, as if
some weird inner force drew them to blood and gore.

She checked her watch. Less than five minutes had
passed since she'd stopped. It seemed more like
thirty. If there was one thing she hated, it was wasting
time. Surely it wouldn't take that much longer before

the police would get the traffic moving again, even if only in one lane.

A tow truck went by about the same time the man who'd gone to take a look at the scene came walking back up the street. Several people in other vehicles either got out to talk to him or rolled down their windows to ask him questions. A small crowd gathered in the middle of the road. Leenie rolled down her window, intending to holler and ask if the guy thought they'd be stuck here much longer, then she heard him say something that made her blood run cold.

"They were putting a gray-haired woman in the ambulance," he said. "It looked bad. Somebody had T-boned her Saturn on the driver's side and crushed it in." He shook his head. "I couldn't make out much, but there was a baby's car seat in back."

Leenie flung open the door, jumped out and ran, leaving the door open, her keys in the ignition and her purse lying on the seat. As she raced past the small crowd, they turned to stare at her, and one person even called out to her. She ignored everyone and everything. By the time she reached the scene of the accident, her breath was labored and her lungs ached. Fear consumed her. When she saw Debra's blue Saturn, she stopped dead still. While she stood there trembling, gasping for air, the ambulance drove past her. She reached out as if she could grab it and stop it.

Andrew! Debra! Her mind screamed their names.

A policeman approached her. "Ma'am, you need to move out of the way."

"Please, I have to—you don't understand."

"Ma'am are you all right?"

"Andrew and Debra. How badly were they hurt?"

"Do you know Mrs. Schmale?" he asked.

Numbness set in. Leenie nodded. "She's my nanny."

"Then you're Dr. Patton?"

"Yes, I'm Lurleen Patton."

The uniformed officer put his arm around Leenie's shoulders and led her out of the street and onto the sidewalk. Without protest, as if in a trance, she went with him.

"Mrs. Schmale is on her way to the hospital," he explained. "She has cuts, bruises, a broken arm and leg and possible internal bleeding. But she was conscious and able to tell us what happened."

"And Andrew?" Leenie asked.

When she noted the peculiar look on the policeman's face, her heart caught in her throat. Was Andrew dead? God, please, no. No! Surely he was all right. Debra always placed him in the regulation seat in the back of her car. And since it had been a driver's side collision...

"Your son...Andrew..." The officer paused, swallowed as if wishing he didn't have to deliver bad news, then said, "Mrs. Schmale told us that a white car came out of nowhere, crashed into her car and the driver jumped out and came to help her. Or so she thought. The driver—a woman—had Mrs. Schmale unlock the doors so she could get in on the other side. Before she realized what was happening, the woman got in the back seat and removed the baby from the car seat. Your nanny thought the woman was simply making sure Andrew was all right. But—"

Leenie swayed toward the officer, then grasped his shoulders and said, "Where is Andrew?"

"The woman took him, put him in her car and drove away," the policeman explained.

"What?"

"We've got an all-points bulletin out for the car—an older model white Buick—and the woman—medium height, weight, short brown hair, sunglasses."

The reality of the situation hit Leenie like a ton of bricks falling on her head. "Andrew was...was..." She couldn't bring herself to say the word, as if not voicing it aloud kept it from being a reality.

"I'm sorry, Dr. Patton, but your baby has been kidnapped."

Two

Leenie couldn't sit still. She felt as if a hundred-mile-an-hour freight train was surging through her. Nerves. Adrenaline. Fear beyond anything she'd ever experienced. Everyone kept telling her to go lie down, take a nap or just rest. Police Chief Ryan Bibb had suggested calling her doctor for a sedative. She knew the man meant well, but why couldn't he—and all the other people who had congregated at her house—understand that she didn't want her senses dulled, that she couldn't sleep or rest. Her baby had been kidnapped. Stolen from her by only God knew what sort of person. She'd overheard the local police surmising about the general identity of Andrew's abductor.

"She's probably some woman who either lost a baby or has a fixation about having a child," Chief Bibb had said. "And if that's the case, she'll take good care of Andrew."

Leenie supposed that believing the kidnapper was taking good care of her baby should be some comfort. It wasn't. Anyone capable of stealing a child had mental problems, whatever their reason.

"Why don't you let me fix you some tea?" Haley Wilson said, as she put her arm around Leenie's shoulder.

The plump brunette, who'd taken over as the manager of WJMM eleven months ago when Elsa Leone—now Elsa Devlin since she'd married—had moved to Knoxville, was a bubbly, energetic woman in her mid-forties and the mother of two teenage sons. From the minute Leenie and she met, they had bonded. Instant friendship. Haley had been the first person she'd called, the first person who'd come to mind when the police had asked her about a friend or family member to stay with her. Haley had dropped everything and rushed to Maysville Memorial, where Leenie had been waiting for Debra to come out of surgery. Haley stayed with her and they had prayed for Debra and for Andrew. Thankfully, Debra had come through the surgery to stop her internal bleeding with flying colors.

"Mrs. Schmale will be in intensive care for the next twenty-four hours," Dr. Brenner had explained. "But I expect a full and speedy recovery."

Knowing that Debra would be all right gave Leenie a great sense of relief. She loved Debra dearly, as a friend and mother figure. The police had said that Debra's ability to accurately describe the kidnapper and the car she'd been driving would be of immeasurable help in locating Andrew.

"Leenie." Haley shook her gently. "Come on in

the kitchen with me. You can sit down long enough for me to fix you some tea."

"I don't want anything to drink."

"Come in the kitchen with me anyway," Haley said. "I'm going to prepare fresh coffee for those FBI people who just arrived and since it's nearly morning, maybe I should offer to make breakfast, too. Why don't you help me?"

Leenie stared at Haley, understanding what she'd said, but not comprehending.

Haley hugged her. "You can't keep pacing the floor and you can't keep going into Andrew's room every ten minutes. You need something to do."

"You're right. Staring at Andrew's crib in the nursery won't make him miraculously appear." Emotion lodged in Leenie's throat. *Don't cry,* she told herself. *Crying isn't going to help. You have to stay strong and in control.*

"They'll find him and bring him home to you." Haley hugged her again, then grasped her hand and tugged. "Come on. Let's make us some tea first, then put on fresh coffee for the others. After that I'll take breakfast orders. And I expect you to eat. Even if it's just a few bites."

Leenie followed her friend into the kitchen, thankful that she had someone with her, someone who understood what it meant to be a mother with a baby boy lost. No, not lost—stolen. Suddenly feeling as if they had become glued to the spot, her feet wouldn't move. The reality of Andrew's disappearance struck her once again, but harder this time, and she sensed that he was being taken farther and farther away from her.

"Leenie?"

"Oh, God, what if—what if—" Tears streamed down her cheeks.

Haley grabbed her and pulled her into her arms. "Cry, dammit. Cry your eyes out."

Leenie fell apart. She sobbed until she was spent. Was it seconds? Minutes? Hours? She didn't know. And all the while Haley held her and stroked her back and murmured soothing, comforting words that Leenie barely heard. As she gulped down the lingering sobs, she lifted her head and looked into Haley's kind hazel eyes.

Haley grasped her shoulders and offered her a fragile smile. "Go wash your face and when you get back, I'll have a cup of tea waiting for you."

Leenie nodded, but before she could turn around, the kitchen door opened and a tall, dark stranger entered. He wasn't one of the local police and he wasn't one of the three FBI agents who had arrived less than an hour ago.

"Dr. Patton?" The golden-eyed man looked right at Leenie.

"Yes."

When he came forward and held out his right hand, she noticed an onyx and diamond ring on his third finger. "I'm Special Agent Dante Moran. I'll be heading up this case."

She shook his hand. Warm. Firm.

"Could we sit and talk, Dr. Patton?" he asked.

"I've talked to the police and to the other FBI agents," she told him. "I don't know what more there is to say."

"No one has discussed possible scenarios with you, have they? Told you what we might be dealing with in Andrew's case?"

She shook her head.

He nodded toward the kitchen table. "Want to sit down?"

"No, I—I can't sit."

"All right." He shrugged. "We aren't sure what we're dealing with here. It's possible that whoever took Andrew simply wanted a baby. If that's—"

"Then she'll probably take good care of him," Leenie said sarcastically.

"Yeah, and I realize that doesn't make you feel any better. But it's better than the other possibilities."

"Which are?"

"He was taken for ransom."

"I'm not rich."

"Not rich, but wealthy," Moran said. "And you are a local celebrity."

"Hell."

"If Andrew was taken for a ransom, we'll be hearing from the kidnapper soon."

"And if he wasn't taken for a ransom?"

"He could have been stolen by someone who intends to sell him. There's a profitable market for stolen babies, especially WASP babies. Blond, blue-eyed. And then there's the other possibility." He looked Leenie square in the eyes. "The worst case scenario is—"

"Dammit, Mr. Moran, do you have to come right out and say it?" Haley practically screamed at the FBI agent.

"Sorry, ma'am." He glanced from Leenie to Haley and then focused on Leenie again. "Rest assured that we're going to do everything in our power to find Andrew and bring him home to you safe and sound."

"Yes, I—I know you will."

"What about Andrew's father?" Moran asked. "I understand you two aren't married, but don't you think that, under the circumstances, you should contact him to let him know his son has been kidnapped?"

Leenie didn't respond; she simply stared into Moran's yellow-brown eyes. After an endless moment, he shrugged. "Why don't you get some rest, Dr. Patton? We can talk again later. Special Agent Walker explained to you the procedure if the phone rings and that we'll screen anyone who comes to the door and—"

"He explained," Haley said.

Moran nodded, then walked out of the kitchen.

Leenie took a deep breath. *What about Andrew's father?* That question repeated itself over and over again inside her head. It wasn't as if she hadn't already asked herself the same thing several times during the night. She had been wrestling with indecision about whether to tell Frank about Andrew's existence since the day her baby was born. But now that Andrew had been abducted, it made the decision all the more difficult. What could she do, call Frank and say, "By the way, we have a baby boy and he's been kidnapped."

"I know what you're thinking," Haley said.

"Yeah, but do you know what I should do?"

"Oh, honey, that's a toughie. What's your heart telling you to do?"

Leenie groaned. "It's telling me that I need Frank, that somehow he can help."

"And what does your brain tell you?"

"That Frank is a Dundee agent, with the resources of the entire agency at his disposal, that he can do things the law can't do and that the Dundee Agency has strong ties to the FBI and—''

''Your heart and your mind are telling you to contact Frank Latimer,'' Haley said.

She sighed. ''How do I tell him about Andrew over the phone?''

''Good question. Is there someone else you could call, someone who could get Frank here under some other pretense so that you can tell him face-to-face?''

''I don't know—'' Leenie paused. ''Well there is Elsa. Maybe my old boss at WJMM, Elsa Devlin, could arrange it. Her husband used to be a Dundee agent. And she and I are good friends.''

''So call Elsa.''

''If I do, she'll come back to Maysville to be with me and she's pregnant and— No, I'm not going to upset Elsa. There was a female Dundee agent named Kate Malone who worked on Elsa's case with Frank. Maybe I could contact her.'' Agitated and uncertain, Leenie paced the floor. ''Oh, hell, maybe I'm complicating this much too much. Maybe I should just call Frank and tell him.''

''Then what are you waiting for?''

''For lightning to strike, I guess. For some sign that calling him is the right thing to do.''

''If you feel you can't call Frank, call this Kate Malone and ask for her help.''

''If she tells Frank that I have a child, he'll know or at the very least suspect the baby is his. Maybe it's better if I don't involve Frank. I don't think I can handle telling him. Not now. Not under these circumstances.''

Frank boarded the Dundee jet, Kate Malone at his side. This was a first for him—flying off on an assignment and not knowing where he was going. Kate had come to his apartment this morning and met the lovely flight attendant, Heather Gant, just as Heather was leaving. Although she hadn't said anything, Kate had lifted a judgmental eyebrow at Frank as the woman passed her in the hall. Ending his months of celibacy was reason for celebration, so he'd been feeling pretty good when Kate showed up.

"Shave and take a shower," Kate had told him. "We're off on an assignment as soon as we can get to the airport."

"No way, I've got vacation time coming."

"It's been canceled. You're needed on this job."

"Can't another agent handle it? Why me?"

"I'll fill you in on the plane," she'd told him. "We have a child kidnapping and the family wants Dundee involved."

"How does the FBI feel about us interfering?"

"Not thrilled. But our old friend Dante Moran is heading up the case, so he knows we won't work at cross purposes with his people."

So, he'd agreed to come along with Kate without putting up too much of a fuss. Although her reasons were apparently personal—and as a general rule none of his fellow agents nosed into other agents' past lives—everyone at Dundee knew that Kate always took a keen interest in any case involving a kidnapped baby. Shortly before leaving her job as Dundee's CEO, Ellen Denby had hired Kate, who was a former Atlanta P.D. officer, just as Ellen had been. And rumor was that they had worked together when Kate was a rookie.

Frank munched on a cheese danish, then washed it

down with black coffee. If he hadn't been such a sucker for a sob story—single mother, overwrought with fear, and an abducted two-month-old boy—he'd be on his way to Sawyer's Hilton Head vacation retreat instead of being midair, flying off on an assignment that was sure to be pure hell on the nerves. Dealing with overwrought mamas wasn't his speciality. He'd leave coddling the abducted kid's mommy to Kate.

He swigged on the coffee, then set aside the dark blue mug with the gold Dundee emblem. "Exactly where are we going?"

"South," Kate replied.

"Could you be more specific?"

"The deep South."

"Why all the secrecy? It's just a child abduction case, isn't it? Nothing hush-hush."

"Yes."

An odd sensation hit him in the gut. Kate had rushed him around so much at his apartment, assuring him she'd give him all the info on their plane trip, that he hadn't actually thought things through. But something didn't feel right about this whole thing.

"We're working on the case as partners," he said. "That means I need to know everything you know."

"Right."

"So fill me in."

"Okay, but I need to tell you things from the beginning. Or at least my beginning."

He nodded.

"Daisy got in touch with me this morning as soon as she arrived at Dundee. A woman named Haley Wilson had phoned her and asked specifically for me. I returned Ms. Wilson's call because she had told

Daisy that we had a mutual acquaintance whose infant son had been kidnapped.''

"So this is personal for you?"

"In a way, but…"

Kate stared at him with a peculiar look of concern in her eyes, and Frank's gut tightened painfully. "But what?"

"Ah, hell, Frank, there's no easy way to say this."

"So, say it, will you?"

"The mutual acquaintance is Dr. Lurleen Patton."

Although he'd thought about her, dreamed about her, cursed her for nearly destroying his love life, no one had mentioned her name in eleven months. "Leenie?"

"Yes, Leenie."

It took him a full minute to wrap his mind around the idea that Leenie had an infant son. "Leenie has a baby?"

"A little boy."

"How old?"

"Two months."

He did the math quickly, but even before adding up eleven months since he'd been with Leenie, he'd known the truth. "The baby's mine."

"Yes."

Then reality sucker punched him. "Leenie's baby has been kidnapped?"

"Yesterday afternoon. Someone crashed their vehicle into the nanny's car. The nanny was injured, but she'll live. The woman who caused the wreck stole the baby from his car seat."

"It is my baby, right?" How was it possible? he asked himself. Yes, he and Leenie had had sex. Repeatedly. But not once had he forgotten to use a condom.

"The lady who called me, this Haley Wilson, is Leenie's best friend and she says the baby is definitely yours."

"Why the hell didn't she—God, Kate, I'm a father."

She reached out and put her hand on his shoulder, then squeezed. "Ms. Wilson said that Leenie is trying very hard to be strong and brave, but she's falling apart. She needs you."

"She needs me now. What about when she first found out she was pregnant? Or when the baby was born?" Frank growled the questions, outrage bringing his blood to a boil.

"And even now, with our child abducted, she's not the one who called and asked for me. Damn her!"

Leenie showered and changed clothes around noon, and at Haley's insistence lay down on the bed. She'd been staring up at the ceiling for the past hour. How could she sleep when she had no idea where Andrew was or what had happened to him? Didn't anyone understand that she was slowly going out of her mind? Although she'd tried to convince herself that it was only a matter of time before the FBI found her baby and brought him home to her, she hadn't been able to escape the wide-awake nightmares that plagued her. What if Andrew had been killed, maybe even tortured?

Keening mournfully, Leenie wrapped her arms around herself and rolled over in the bed. *Oh, God, please take care of Andrew. Don't let anyone hurt him.* Tears gathered in her eyes. She swallowed hard.

A sharp knock on the bedroom door gained her immediate attention. She sat straight up. "Yes?"

"Leenie, there's someone here to see you," Haley said through the closed door.

"I don't want to see anyone. Please tell whoever it is that—"

The door flew open. Frank Latimer stormed into her bedroom. Frank? Frank! What was he doing here? How had he found out about—?

He marched across the room to the bed, reached down, grabbed her by the arm and yanked her to her feet. They stood there staring at each other. Leenie's heartbeat accelerated at an alarming speed.

"Why the hell didn't you let me know I had a son?" he demanded.

Leenie trembled from head to toe, but she kept her gaze locked with his. "How did you—who told you about Andrew?"

"I did." Haley stepped into the bedroom, Kate Malone directly behind her. "Well, actually, I spoke to Ms. Malone and she told him about Andrew and what had happened."

"Leenie, we're here to help," Kate said. "You have all of Dundee's resources and manpower at your service. We're going to work with Moran…with the FBI to find your little boy." Kate came over and grasped Frank's arm. "And despite his less than pleasant greeting, Frank is here to help you." She shook his arm. "Aren't you, Frank?"

He broke eye contact with Leenie long enough to confront Kate. "How about you two let me talk to Leenie alone, without an audience."

"Is that all right with you?" Haley asked Leenie. She nodded.

Haley glared at Frank. "I'm the one responsible for your knowing about Andrew. Don't make me regret what I did." She hurriedly left the room.

After letting go of his arm, Kate hesitated. "The absolute worst thing that can happen when a child is kidnapped is for her—or his—parents to blame each other and be at each other's throats. What Leenie needs right now, Frank, is your understanding and your support."

He didn't reply, but he released his tenacious hold on Leenie's arm. Kate gave him a warning glare before leaving them alone. For several minutes the silence between them pulsated throughout the bedroom. A bedroom in which they had made mad, passionate love on more than one occasion. She couldn't help remembering and her body warmed as those luscious memories encompassed her. Frank's hard body pressing her into the mattress as he plunged into her. The feel of his strong arms holding her. His moist lips on hers, at her breasts. His fingers caressing, probing, tantalizing. For a millisecond she stopped breathing.

"I spoke to Dante Moran…briefly," Frank said, his voice tight and controlled. "The local police found the vehicle that crashed into your nanny's car. It was abandoned outside of town. Naturally there was no sign of the baby. Our baby."

"His name is Andrew," Leenie said.

He clenched his jaw, then said, "My middle name."

She nodded. "Andrew Latimer Patton."

Frank huffed, then frowned and shifted his shoulders. "Damn, Leenie, why didn't you tell me?"

"I don't know," she said. "Pride maybe. Too proud to ask for your help when I was perfectly capable of taking care of myself and a child without a father. Or maybe I was scared that you'd do the honorable thing and ruin all our lives. I don't know. We weren't even a couple, not really. We had a fling. No strings attached. We used protection. You left and never called or—''

"I thought about calling," he told her.

Had he? she wondered. She wanted to believe him, but it really didn't matter. He might have thought about it, but he hadn't called. Not once in nearly a year. "Admit it, Frank, if Haley hadn't called Kate and you didn't know about Andrew, you'd never have gotten in touch with me."

"We can't know that for sure, can we? Besides, that's a moot point now anyway."

"Actually my not telling you about your child is a moot point." She wanted to touch Frank, to put her arms around him and beg him to hold her. "Until we find Andrew, nothing else matters."

"You're right. Finding our son is our only concern. Everything else can be sorted out later, once we bring him home."

"For what it's worth..." she paused and looked right at Frank "...I'm glad you're here."

Three

Frank had left Leenie in her bedroom and gone through the house, out the back door and onto the porch. For late November, it was unseasonably warm. Probably somewhere in the high sixties and not a rain cloud in the sky. He'd gotten away from Leenie as fast as he could because he'd sensed that she had wanted him to put his arms around her and hold her. But he hadn't. He couldn't. And not just because he was angry with her, that a part of him wanted to wring that long, smooth neck of hers for keeping his son a secret from him. He knew that if he touched her, she'd work that crazy magic spell on him and make him want to stay with her, hold on to her, make love to her and never let her go. When he'd left Maysville eleven months ago after his assignment ended, he'd sworn he'd never look back. The way Leenie turned him inside out had scared the hell out of him. He'd decided a long time ago that no woman was ever again going to do a number on him. No way was he going to let Leenie twist him around her little finger.

Yeah, well, Frank old buddy, maybe Leenie knew exactly how you felt. It wasn't as if he'd made a big secret of not wanting anything beyond a brief affair. He had told her he was not the type of guy for a committed relationship. Is it any wonder that when she found out she was pregnant, she didn't pick up the phone and call him? She probably had serious doubts he'd be thrilled to hear he was a father-to-be.

Okay, so maybe he had to accept part of the blame. Maybe he shouldn't take all his anger out on her.

The last time Frank had allowed anything to tear him apart inside had been twelve years ago when he'd walked in on his wife in bed with another man. They'd been married for two years and he'd been fool enough to think they were happy. He had been happy. Apparently Rita hadn't been. She'd decided she wanted more than Frank could give her and zeroed in on her married boss, a guy twice her age. Even now, after all these years, Frank could still remember how it felt seeing their naked bodies writhing on the bed. His bed, the one he'd slept in every night with Rita. And he could almost feel the power in the repeated punches he'd inflicted on Rodney Klyce. He'd beaten the hell out of the guy, but Klyce hadn't pressed charges. He'd wanted the whole thing kept quite because of his wife. But before Frank had packed his bags and left town, he'd called Mrs. Klyce. A bitter, vengeful thing to have done, but he'd never regretted it. He'd later heard she'd divorced Klyce and taken him for half his net worth. He'd also heard that Rita married Klyce, then divorced him a few years later and moved on to greener pastures. By now she'd probably gone through half a dozen husbands, and he could truthfully say he didn't give a damn.

He'd been a fool about Rita, a brown-eyed beauty with flaming red hair. She'd made him forget all about his solemn vow to never marry, to never repeat his parents' mistake. Their battle royale divorce when he was twelve should have proven to him how easily love can turn to hate and that eventually hate evolved into apathy. But learning that lesson a second time—firsthand—had seared it into both his conscious and subconscious. Love affairs were okay. Love was not. After Rita, he'd shut himself off from anything other than lust and sex. He'd thought that was all it had been with Leenie. Even when he'd realized he couldn't get her out of his mind, couldn't forget her, he'd halfway convinced himself that what he really couldn't forget was the fantastic sex.

You don't love her, he told himself. *You aren't capable of love.*

But the fact that he'd gotten her pregnant and she'd given birth to his child bonded them forever, marriage or no marriage. He had a son. A two-month-old son.

Frank cursed under his breath, then pounded his fist against the doorframe. He'd never given fatherhood a thought. When he'd sworn off love and marriage, naturally he'd assumed there wouldn't be any kids in his future and that had been fine with him. He was forty damn years old. Too old to become a first-time father.

The more he thought about the situation, the more he came to realize why Leenie hadn't told him about Andrew. If he'd been Leenie, he wouldn't have called him with the news. He was lousy father material. He needed to talk to her, apologize for acting like a jerk.

The woman had been traumatized enough by her baby's kidnapping and all he'd done was add to that trauma.

Just as he reached out to open the back door, Kate and Moran came outside onto the porch. He could tell by their expressions that the news wasn't good.

"What's happened?" Frank asked.

"Nothing new," Kate said. "But Dante has some information he's willing to share with you, not as Andrew's father, but as a Dundee agent who has certain government clearances and is deemed totally trustworthy."

"Cut the crap and lay it on the line," Frank told her.

"It's good news and bad news," she said.

"We're fairly certain we know who kidnapped your son," Special Agent Moran said.

"What?" Frank glared at Moran.

"Not the name of a person, but an organization," Kate said. "The good news is that the FBI is reasonably certain the woman who stole Andrew isn't some nutcase who'll kill him or keep him for herself."

"And just what makes the Feds so certain?" He looked to Moran for the answer.

"We unearthed information about an infant abduction ring several years ago," Moran said. "We're not sure how long it's been in operation, but we suspect at least ten years. We're on the verge of setting up a sting operation that will lead us right to the top, to the people making big money by stealing Caucasian babies and selling them to unsuspecting couples who'll gladly pay a hundred thousand or more for a cuddly blue-eyed, blond-haired baby."

"Hell. Are you telling me that you think Andrew was stolen by this baby abduction ring?"

"The odds are pretty high that he'll soon be sold to the highest bidder."

"Son of a bitch." Frank glowered at Kate. "And this is the good news?"

"At least there's a good chance they'll take care of him because he's worth a great deal of money to them."

In desperation Frank said, "What if we run an ad in the paper offering more than a hundred grand for Andrew's safe return?"

"These people aren't going to take any chances on getting caught," Moran said. "Selling these kids to adoptive parents is easy money because it's safe. The people who adopt these babies aren't going to ask too many questions about where their baby came from, now are they?"

"How close are you guys to nabbing them?"

"You know I can't tell you the details." Moran felt in his coat pocket, then patted his shirt pocket before letting his hand fall to his side. "I quit smoking nearly a year ago, but I can't kick the habit of reaching for one now and again."

"How close?" Frank repeated.

"Close."

"I want in on the sting."

"You know that's not possible."

"Who are these people and where do we find them?" Frank caught the sidelong glances Kate and Moran exchanged. "There's a good chance Andrew will be the next baby up on the auction block, so why not send me and Kate in as prospective parents?"

"We've got federal agents who can do that. Besides, you're the kidnapped boy's father. You're too close to this to—"

Frank grabbed Moran by his lapels and hauled him close so that they were eye-to-eye.

"If it were your kid, what would you do?"

Moran, cool as a cucumber, looked directly at Frank and said, "I'd want to go in myself and get my child and then I'd want to kill every bastard involved in the abduction ring...kill them with my bare hands."

Frank loosened his hold on Moran's suit, then released the lapels and took a deep breath. "And some stupid federal agent would stop you."

Moran's lips twitched with a hint of a smile. "You know it."

"How much can I tell Leenie?" Frank asked.

"Tell her about the abduction ring and our suspicions that Andrew was stolen by these slimeballs, but that's it. If and when we make a move, you can tell her afterward, hopefully when we bring her son home to her."

"She'll be mad as hell at all of us," Frank said.

"After the way you treated her in there, I'd say she's already mad as hell at you," Kate told him. "Maybe you should go back inside and talk to her, even apologize."

"Maybe you're right."

Kate smiled. "Could be there's hope for you yet, Latimer."

Leenie ran a comb through her hair, then opened her jewelry case and removed a pair of gold and diamond earrings. She'd been wearing these the first time she'd seen Frank. He'd come into WJMM as part

of the Dundee team sent to Maysville to protect Elsa
Leone against death threats nearly a year ago. He and
Kate had been the investigative team and they'd set
up shop in Elsa's office in the WJMM studio complex. The minute she'd met Frank, she'd wanted him.
And she'd had him in record time. She had thought
he'd be her first one-night stand; instead their encounter had turned out to be the first time she'd ever
had sex with someone she'd just met, someone little
more than a stranger. But with Frank it had seemed
right not to wait. The sex had been incredible. They'd
set the sheets on fire and sent off skyrockets. And the
more they had sex, the more they'd wanted it. They
couldn't get enough of each other.

Leenie slipped the earrings on, then slid her fingers
down the side of her neck, remembering the feel of
Frank's big, rough fingers caressing her.

While she stood staring at herself in the mirror, her
eyes glazed over with memories, Haley came in and
walked up behind her. "You haven't eaten enough to
keep a bird alive. Why don't you let me make you a
sandwich."

"Food won't help," Leenie said. "I feel as if I eat
a bite, I'll throw it up."

"How did things go with Frank?"

"You don't want to know."

"What did he do?"

"He hates me." Leenie sighed. "And I can't blame
him. He had every right to know about his son. He
doesn't understand why I didn't tell him I was pregnant."

A deep male voice said, "Yes, he does understand."

Leenie gasped when she saw Frank's reflection in

the mirror. Haley turned around and gave him a withering glare as she moved past him toward the door.

Haley paused, glanced over her shoulder and said, "See if you can get her to eat something. And if you say or do anything to upset her, you'll answer to me."

The minute Haley closed the door, Frank came up behind Leenie. Her breath caught in her throat. A part of her still wanted his arms around her; another part of her wanted to tell him to go away and leave her alone. She simply stood there, those stupid diamond earrings glimmering in the fading late afternoon sunlight coming through the sheer window curtains. Why had she put on these earrings? Had she thought he'd actually remember her wearing them?

"I'm sorry," he said.

She looked at his reflection in the mirror and plainly saw the sincerity of his words in the expression on his face. And in his eyes. Those stormy-sea gray eyes that spoke volumes.

Emotion tightened her throat. She couldn't speak, so she nodded.

He touched her then. Those big, hard hands tenderly clutched her shoulders. *Don't fall apart,* she told herself. *Don't crumble and fall into his arms. He's not here for you. He came because of Andrew.*

"I know you had your reasons for not telling me you were pregnant," he said. "You probably figured I wouldn't relish the news of impending fatherhood."

She inhaled deeply and exhaled slowly.

His hands tightened ever so slightly on her shoulders. "After the way we ended things, you had no reason to think I'd want to be a part of Andrew's life."

"I should have told you," she finally managed to say.

"It doesn't matter now. Finding Andrew and bringing him home is what matters. And I swear to you, Leenie, I'll move heaven and earth to do that."

She swallowed the tears choking her. Of its own accord her body swayed backward toward his and the minute it did, he slid his hands downward from her shoulders and wrapped his arms around her. Her back pressed against his chest and for the first time since Andrew had been kidnapped, she felt a sense of hope. Crazy as the notion was, her heart believed that Frank could keep his promise to bring their baby home to her.

"I love him so," she said. "He's everything… to…me." Her shaky voice grew softer with each word as she tried in vain to keep from crying. "At first I couldn't…cry. Now I—I can't…seem…to stop…crying."

Hugging her comfortingly, he lowered his head and pressed his cheek against her temple. "I wish I could cry. God knows I feel like it."

Startled by his comment, she stiffened in his arms. Frank Latimer crying? She couldn't imagine it. Was he saying that he cared about Andrew, even loved him? Was it possible that he was actually pleased about having a son? Or was his reaction strictly impersonal, the kind any normal person would have after learning a two-month-old baby had been kidnapped?

"I know what you're thinking," he said, his voice husky with emotion. "You're wondering what kind of man I am, if I'm pleased to be a father or horrified. You're thinking how dare he care now, after the fact.

Why didn't he call me after he left Maysville nearly a year ago? He's a day late and a dollar short.''

As the tension drained from her body, she allowed his strength to support her. Instinct told her that despite their past history, Frank was a man she could lean on, a man she could count on when the chips were down. And God knew she needed somebody strong right now, someone who felt what she felt—the panic and terror, the excruciating pain. Only Andrew's father could even begin to understand the depth of her feelings.

"How do you feel about having a child?" She avoided looking at his reflection in the mirror. She knew that no matter what he said, his true reaction would show on his face. She'd learned that much about him during their brief interlude. Frank Latimer did not have a poker face.

He turned her in his arms. "Look at me, Leenie."

She lifted her gaze to meet his and saw confusion in his eyes, as well as concern.

"I'm not sure how I feel," he admitted. "I never thought about being a father. I knew, after my divorce, that I'd never get married again. And I'm just old-fashioned enough to think a guy should get married before he fathers a child. I don't have unsafe sex. You know that."

"Condoms aren't foolproof," she told him. "And I wasn't on the pill. Most doctors recommend another form of birth control for women after they turn thirty-five."

"You don't have to explain. We thought we were being careful. Responsible. Accident's happen."

"Is that how you think of Andrew, as an accident?" Heat suffused her face as her temper rose.

"Don't put words in my mouth. All I'm saying is that Andrew's conception was an accident. I just found out today that I'm a father. Give me some time to figure out what I think about having a child. You had nine months of pregnancy and two months with Andrew to figure out how you feel. Did you know immediately when you found out you were pregnant that you wanted the child, that you loved him?"

Well, he had her there. No, of course she hadn't known immediately that she loved and wanted her baby. When she'd read the home pregnancy test, she'd panicked. And when the doctor had confirmed her condition, she'd stayed in a state of shock for days. She had even considered an abortion. But only for about two minutes.

"You're right. I was being unfair putting you on the spot that way."

He cupped her face with his hands. "I do know this—I care about Andrew. And I'll do whatever it takes to bring our son home to you. Once he's back in your arms, we'll figure out where to go from there."

"Fair enough." She swallowed fresh tears.

"I realize we're little more than strangers to each other. We had a whirlwind love affair and we spent most of our time making love, not getting acquainted."

She nodded.

"I'd like to learn more about Andrew, if you're willing to talk to me about him. It might help you. Hell, it might help both of us. But if you'd rather not, it's okay."

She pulled away from Frank, walked across the room and picked up the most recent photograph of her baby. "This was taken a few weeks ago. It's a picture of him I took with my digital camera. I enlarged it and framed it." She held it out to Frank.

He didn't move for a couple of minutes, as if he were afraid of the picture. Was he wondering how his first glimpse of his son would affect him?

"He's asleep in this picture, so you can't see his eyes." She moved toward Frank, the framed photograph in her hand. "He has blue eyes, like mine. And blond hair. Not much hair, mostly just baby-fine fluff." *He has your mouth, your chin and your hands and feet,* she wanted to say, but didn't. "He's big for his age. He weighed nine pounds, five ounces, when he was born."

Frank glanced down at the picture, then reached out and took it. He stared at the photo for what seemed like forever, then smiled and said, "He looks like you. Lucky kid."

Leenie clenched her teeth to keep from crying.

"I guess he'll grow up to be tall, huh, since I'm six-three and you're—what?—five-nine or ten." Frank looked at her.

She nodded. "He has big hands and big feet. Long toes and long fingers." She cast her gaze on Frank's hand holding the frame.

"Like me." He looked at Andrew's picture again, then handed it back to Leenie.

She placed the frame on the bedside table and slumped down on the edge of the bed. When she turned back to Frank, she noticed he was headed toward the door. *Don't leave me,* she wanted to cry, *please don't leave me.*

He glanced back at her. "I need to get my bag out

of the rental car. I'm going to stay here with you until
we find Andrew, if that's all right.''

Her heart soared. "Yes. Yes, it's all right with
me.''

He offered her a forced smile, then opened the
door.

"Thank you," she called.

He paused momentarily, but didn't turn or speak;
then he left.

When Frank brought his bag in, Haley Wilson
stopped him in the foyer. "Are you planning on stay-
ing?''

"Yeah.''

"Good.''

"Look, Ms. Wilson, if you have something to say
to me, just say it.''

"All right. Leenie is one of the strongest, most independent women I know. But she's vulnerable right
now. Her whole life is hanging in the balance because
Andrew *is* her life. I don't know if you can understand
that, but as a mother myself, I do. So, no matter what
your own feelings are or how you plan to deal with
things when y'all get Andrew back, right now, Leenie
needs you. She needs your support and your comfort.''

"I agree.''

Haley stared at him, a puzzled expression on her
face. "She hasn't slept since the night before last and
she hasn't eaten since lunch yesterday. I've gotten her
to drink a little tea, but that's all. Do you think you
could get her to eat?''

"Is there any cheesecake in the house?" Frank

asked, remembering how they had devoured cheese-cake at dawn, after a marathon lovemaking session.

Haley cocked her head sideways and smiled. "You do know a little something about her, don't you? As for the cheesecake—I had my husband stop by the bakery and drop one by here a little while ago."

Frank dumped his bag in the corner of the foyer. "I'll take her a piece and make sure she eats it." He looked directly at Leenie's friend. "I'm going to take care of her. I promise."

This woman had no way of knowing that Frank Latimer didn't make promises easily, that when he made one, he kept it.

Five minutes later, Frank entered Leenie's bed-room. He carried two slices of cheesecake and two cups of hot tea on a tray. Leenie glanced up at him from where she still sat on the edge of the bed. She clutched a damp, wrinkled handkerchief in her hand.

"Snack time." He walked over, placed the tray on the bed and sat beside her. "Cheesecake and hot tea. Remember?"

"Yes, I remember, but I'm surprised that you do."

He lifted one plate and fork and handed them to her. "Eat up."

"Frank, I'm not—"

"Eat." He picked up the other plate, sliced off a large chunk of cheesecake and slid it into his mouth. After chewing and swallowing, he sighed dramati-cally. "Nothing better than cheesecake, except—"

"Sex," she finished his sentence.

Grinning, he took a second bite before placing his plate back on the tray. He eased his hand under her hand to support her plate, then lifted her fork and cut off a piece of the cheesecake and lifted it to her mouth. She parted her lips; he slid the cheesecake into her mouth. As soon as she finished one bite, he gave her another, and then another—slowly, patiently—until three-fourths of her slice was gone.

"I can't eat anymore," she told him.

He set her plate on the tray, then handed her the tea. While she sipped the tea, he drank his, watching her all the while. After she drained her cup, he removed the tray from the bed and placed it on the floor.

Leenie was dead on her feet, worn out from lack of sleep and the stress of not knowing where Andrew was or if he was all right. Frank realized she needed more than cheesecake and tea. She needed to rest. He scooted up in her bed until his back hit the headboard, then he reached out, grasped Leenie's hand and tugged on it urging her to join him. They sat side-by-side in her bed, their backs resting against the headboard. Frank put his arm around her shoulders and cuddled her against him.

"Would you believe I had blond hair and blue eyes when I was a baby?" he said.

"What?" Turning her head sideways, she glanced over at him.

"I had blond hair and blue eyes like Andrew. So his eyes could turn gray later on and his hair might not stay blond like yours."

She laid her head on his shoulder. "I was bald when I was born. Well, actually, I think I had some white fuzz, but it wasn't much. I have a couple of baby pictures that a distant relative sent me when I contacted her after I grew up and started searching for any family I might have."

"That's right. You grew up in foster homes, didn't you?"

"Uh-huh. After my parents died, I got shuffled from one foster home to another, until I was fifteen and wound up with Debra and Jerry Schmale."

"Debra? The same Debra who's Andrew's nanny?"

"That's right." Leenie yawned.

"How's she doing after her surgery?"

"I spoke to her doctor earlier today and he said she should be able to go into a private room tomorrow. Debra's a wonderful person, the only real mother-figure I ever had that I can remember. My own mother died when I was four and I can barely remember her."

"I grew up in a fairly conventional family. Mom, dad and an older sister. Then when I was twelve my parents divorced. Ripped us to shreds. My sister went with Mom and I lived with Dad."

"It must have been difficult for you."

"Pure hell. You see, my mother had taken a lover and my father wanted to make her pay for her sins." Frank glanced at Leenie, her eyes shut, her lips slightly parted, her breathing soft and even.

"Did you hate your mother after that?" Leenie asked, her voice hushed.

"Yeah, I hated her for a long, long time, but that's all in the past now," Frank said, looking at the way Leenie's eyelids closed and realizing what she needed was sleep. He moved on to more mundane topics and Leenie melted against him as she began drifting off to sleep. He kept talking quietly until he knew she was fast asleep, then he eased her down into the bed so that her head rested in his lap. He pulled the folded quilt at the foot of the bed up and over her. While she slept, he watched her. Drank his fill of her.

He admitted to himself that he'd missed Leenie while they'd been apart. He'd missed seeing her, talking to her, having sex with her. She was the first woman since Rita who'd stirred something inside him other than lust.

But you don't love her, Frank told himself. *She's special. She's the mother of your child. But you do not love her.*

He caressed her hair and the side of her face tenderly. ''Get some rest, Slim. I'm here now. You won't have to go through this alone.''

Four

Andrew dangled helpless over the deep, dark well, a large hand holding him by the nape of his tiny neck. The hand loosened its grip and released the baby. His frightened cries echoed in the blackness as he fell down, down, down. God, no…no…no! Leenie tried to reach out and grab her son, but her efforts were useless. All she could do was scream in terror.

"Leenie…Leenie…wake up."

Strong masculine hands grasped her shoulders and shook her gently. She tried to fight him, fear spiraling through her alarmingly.

"Slim, it's me—Frank. Wake up. You were having a nightmare."

She opened her eyes suddenly and stared into Frank Latimer's concerned gray eyes.

"Oh, Frank, it was awful. Someone dropped Andrew into a deep well. He was crying...crying for me.''

Frank pulled her up off the bed and into his arms, his strength enveloping her. She clung to him, her mind and nerves rioting. ''It was just a bad dream,'' he told her.

''I know.'' She burrowed her head against his shoulder and closed her eyes. ''But he's out there—lost.'' She lifted her head and stared at Frank. ''We have to find him. Please, tell me that we can save him. Make me believe that he's not lost to me forever.''

Frank brushed loose strands of hair out of her face. His hand lingered, his fingertips caressed. And then he withdrew. She felt the emotional withdrawal as keenly as the physical release. He eased out of bed, his back to her, and said nothing for several awkward minutes.

''Frank?''

''I'll do everything I can, but...'' He turned halfway toward her, his jaw tense, his gaze unfocused as he glared off into nothingness. ''I don't make promises I can't keep. I've already sworn to you that I would move heaven and earth to bring Andrew home, and I meant it. I'll do everything humanly possible. But the honest truth is that even though I'd do anything to rescue Andrew, I can't promise you that I can bring him back to you safe and sound.''

Her heart lurched, then sank. This wasn't what she'd wanted to hear. She had thought he would reinforce his earlier vow to rescue Andrew and had longed to hear him say those comforting words. Even knowing Frank wasn't a miracle worker, she believed in him. He was her last best hope.

"What time is it?" she asked, needing the mundane to keep her sane, to take her mind out of the horrific abyss that sucked her in and kept repeating terrifying mental images of her baby's death.

Frank glanced at his wristwatch. "Nearly four-thirty."

"I slept quite a while." As she stretched, every muscle in her body cried from the tension that had played havoc on her physically, mentally and emotionally.

"You needed the rest. Your friend Haley said you haven't slept since Andrew's abduction." Frank glanced at the stacked empty dishes on the tray. "You should try to eat some supper later on."

"You're beginning to sound like a mother hen—telling me to rest and to eat."

"It's the training," he told her. "Part of the regimen for looking after someone is making sure they take care of themselves. A Dundee agent is an all-around bodyguard. He or she tries to not only protect the client, but see to their well-being."

"And am I a client? Is that how you think of me now?"

"You're putting words in my mouth again, Slim."

"I'm only interpreting what I hear you say."

"You're misinterpreting," he said. "And you're being argumentative. Why? Are you angry with me for some reason?"

Was she angry with him? Yes. No. Maybe.

Leenie got out of bed, rubbed the back of her sore neck and slipped on her shoes. Had Frank taken her shoes off after she'd fallen asleep? More of his all-around bodyguard duties? Was that it—the reason she suddenly felt so hostile toward him? Because he'd acted as if his kindness to her wasn't anything personal?

"I'm angry with the world right now," she admitted. "Besides, I believe that should be my question, not yours. After all, you're the one who has every right to be angry and upset with me for keeping Andrew's existence a secret from you."

He shot her a quick glance, then looked away before he replied, "I told you before that now is not the time for us to be at cross purposes, that once Andrew is safely home will be time enough to—"

"To what? For you to tell me what you really think, how you really feel?"

"I don't know how I feel. I don't want to dig too deep right now." He looked at her. "You're hurting enough for both of us. I need to stay as detached and as unemotional as possible."

"Can you do that? Can you be unemotional when it comes to Andrew?"

Could he actually remain detached where his own child was concerned? If so, then he certainly wasn't the man she'd thought he was. But then again, she didn't really know Frank Latimer. He was a stranger with whom she'd had a passionate fling. She knew without a doubt that he was an incredible lover. Considerate. Attentive. She knew he liked his coffee black, his whiskey straight and his loving frequent. But beyond the obvious, she knew nothing, except what little he'd told her today. And the same held true for him—he didn't know who the real Lurleen Patton was.

When the silence between them became more than she could bear, she said, "Can't you answer me?"

"What do you want me to say? Yes, I care about

my son. I'm not a heartless bastard. But for God's sake, Leenie, I haven't even seen him or touched him or held him. And I've known that I'm a father for only a few hours.''

"I'm sorry. I—"

"No, I'm sorry," he told her. "Sorry I can't say whatever it is you need for me to say. But the more unemotional and detached I can be, the clearer my thinking, the more logical I'll act and react. Don't you see—"

"I see. I see a man who's afraid to feel. You don't want to love Andrew. You don't want to love anybody because sometimes love hurts.''

Clenching her teeth in an effort not to burst into fresh tears, Leenie rushed toward the door, wanting to get away from Frank. But he caught up with her just as she reached for the doorknob. He grasped her arm. She stopped and glared at him.

"There it is again," he said. "Anger. You're angry with me. Want to tell me why? I've tried to be honest with you, so how about being honest with me?"

She jerked her arm loose and took a step backward, but she kept her gaze boldly glued to his. "You want honesty? All right. I kept Andrew a secret from you because I didn't know how you'd react. I was half afraid you'd want to take him away from me and half afraid you'd tell me you didn't give a damn. But your reaction is somewhere in between and I can't figure you out. I feel like a fool for having gotten myself pregnant by a man I don't even know. And a part of me is angry because on some completely stupid female level I needed you to care—really care. Not just about Andrew, but about me. I needed you to *not* be detached and unemotional.''

They stood there staring at each other for several minutes until the silence stretched tautly and the tension mounted.

A solid, repetitive knock on the door snapped the tension and ended the silence.

"Frank?" Kate Malone called.

Frank opened the door. "Yeah, what is it?"

"Moran wants to talk to you and Dr. Patton."

"Has something happened?" Leenie asked.

"No bad news," Kate said. "He just wants to go over some things with y'all."

Frank held the door open while Leenie walked into the hall and joined Kate, then he followed behind them, down the hall and into the living room. Only Dante Moran occupied the room, which made Leenie wonder where the other FBI agents were and if Haley was still here.

"Come on in," Moran said. "Please. We need to talk."

"Is Haley—?"

"Mrs. Wilson went home," Kate replied. "She said if you need her, to call her. The house was getting a little crowded, what with two Dundee agents and several FBI agents."

"Where are the other agents?" Leenie asked.

"From here on out, they'll work in shifts. We have your phone tapped and we're fully prepared to act at a moment's notice," Moran said. "The crucial first twenty-four hours has ended." When Leenie stared at him quizzically, he continued. "If the kidnapper is going to demand a ransom, the family usually hears something within the first twenty-four hours."

Kate answered Leenie's next question before she asked it. "Which means that more than likely Andrew was not kidnapped for ransom money, but for another reason."

"How will we know if the woman who stole him kept him, that she wanted him for herself?" Wasn't that the best case scenario for a kidnapping? Leenie wondered.

"We can't know for sure." Moran cut a sideways glance at Frank. "Did you tell her about the abduction ring?"

"What abduction ring?" Leenie's heart skipped a beat.

Frank shook his head. "I didn't get a chance to tell her."

"What abduction ring?" Leenie repeated her question.

"The bureau is aware that there is an infant abduction ring operating in the South and it is possible that your baby was taken in order to sell him," Moran told her.

"Sell him? You mean—"

"Sell him to people who desperately want to adopt a child," Kate explained. "Unfortunately there is a shortage of white infants and some people are willing to pay an exorbitant amount in order to procure a child through any means necessary."

"They're willing to buy a child that's been stolen from a loving home?" Leenie looked from Kate to Moran, but she couldn't bring herself to make eye contact with Frank.

"In all fairness, these people are told that the children have been willingly given up by parents who don't want them and these adoptive parents want a child so much that they kid themselves into believing whatever they need to believe." Kate put her hand on Leenie's shoulder. "Don't give up hope. Don't ever give up hope."

Having noted a peculiar tone in Kate's voice, Leenie studied her for several moments. The two women exchanged silent confidences and unspoken pain. Without truly understanding, Leenie knew that at some time in her life Kate Malone had suffered an intolerable loss, perhaps the loss of a child. She reached up and covered Kate's hand with her own. "I won't give up." She squeezed Kate's hand, then turned to Frank. "From now on, please don't keep anything from me. I'm not some weak, trembling female who can't handle the truth. Yes, I've been crying a great deal and I'm scared out of my mind and I'll gladly lean on anybody who'll let me. But do not treat me as if I'm a child myself. Do I make myself clear?"

Frank glowered at her for a split second. "Yeah. Crystal clear." Looking as if she'd slapped him, Frank darted a glance from Moran to Kate, then grumbled, "I need a breath of fresh air."

"And I need a smoke," Moran said, "but I'll settle for some of that cold fresh air outside."

As soon as the two men disappeared into the kitchen, presumably to go out on the porch or into the backyard, Kate turned to Leenie and offered a comforting smile.

"Cut Frank some slack," Kate advised. "Basically he's a good guy. It's just that discovering he's a father has thrown him for a loop. You may think Andrew's kidnapping isn't as hard on him as it is you, but it probably is. Maybe even more so."

"How do you figure that?"

"Because he's thinking that if—just if, mind you—

Andrew isn't rescued, then he'll never see his son or hold him or get the chance to love him.''

''And I have seen him and held him and loved him.''

''Look, this is none of my business. Not really.'' Kate clicked her tongue. ''Want some advice from a busybody?''

Leenie wanted to ask Kate the question that hung heavily between them—did you lose a child?—but she didn't ask. ''I'm taking my frustration out on Frank, aren't I? And I shouldn't. Isn't that what you were going to say?''

''Something like that.'' Kate nodded. ''Frank's not the enemy.''

''Who is the enemy? Someone who might still call and ask for ransom? Some crazy woman who stole my baby for herself? Some maniac who kills babies? Or the money-hungry abduction ring who steals babies and sells them?''

''We don't know which. Not yet.''

''When will we know?''

Kate closed her eyes for a millisecond as if she'd suddenly experienced a pain too agonizing to bear, then she took a deep, cleansing breath and replied, ''I don't know the answer to that either. We may find out tomorrow. Or next week. Or maybe never.'' She reached out and grabbed Leenie's shoulders. ''But no matter how long it takes, do not give up. Don't ever let anyone convince you to give up.''

Before Leenie could respond, Kate released her and walked away, mumbling something about needing to go to the bathroom as she disappeared down the hall.

Leenie sank down into the nearest chair, leaned over, propped her elbows on her knees and cupped her face with her open palms. Sitting there alone, the house eerily quiet, she said one more prayer.

Please, dear God, keep Andrew safe and bring him home to me. Home to me and Frank.

Kate handed Moran a cup of coffee, then poured one for herself and sat down across the kitchen table from him. "Where did Frank go?" she asked.

"For a walk down the street. He said to tell you he'd be back in a little while."

Kate studied Dante Moran, a dark, compellingly handsome man, with danger written all over him. She didn't think she'd ever met such a cool character and she'd known her share of self-confident, powerful men. Her ex-husband had been rich, powerful and arrogant in a way only someone born and bred into wealth and power can be. Most of the time she managed not to think about Trent Winston. Trenton Bayard Winston IV. But this kidnapping case had brought back all the old and painful memories. It was only natural that she'd think about Trent, wasn't it, and wonder how he was doing? She hadn't seen him in nearly eleven years. Not since—

"How's she holding up?" Moran nodded toward the living room.

"Dr. Patton? She's doing okay, considering her child is missing and that child's father is trying to help her and probably saying and doing all the wrong things."

"Men are like that." Moran's lips twitched with a hint of humor.

"Yes, you are. All of you."

"Including your ex?"

"How'd you know— You didn't, did you? Not until I reacted. And before you ask, I do not want to talk about him or about it.''

''It?'' Moran cocked an inquisitive eyebrow.

''It. The divorce. What about you, Moran—got an ex-wife and a less than pleasant divorce you don't want to talk about?''

''No marriages. No divorces.''

''Hmm-mmm.''

''And before you ask—''

''Why is a guy who's decidedly over thirty-five never been married?''

''Yeah, that's the question I don't want you to ask.'' He actually grinned.

''Being a woman, my guess would be either unrequited love and you're still hoping to eventually woo and win her…or you loved and lost and—'' A flicker of something incomprehensible danced in Moran's black eyes, coming and going so quickly that she could have imagined it. But she hadn't. Loved and lost. That was it. Moran's *it* that he couldn't bear to talk about, the way her divorce from Trent was her unbearable *it*.

Moran sipped on his coffee. Kate did the same.

The phone rang and both of them tensed.

He got up and rushed into the living room. Kate quickly followed. Leenie stood by the phone, allowing it to ring, and looked to Moran for direction the minute she saw him. He nodded and motioned for her to answer the phone.

Although Leenie's hand trembled as she lifted the receiver, her voice was steady when she said, ''This is Dr. Lurleen Patton.'' Tears gathered in the corners of her eyes. She gasped, then responded, ''No, thank you, I'm not interested in a free vacation." She slammed down the receiver.

Kate released the breath she'd unknowingly been holding. "It's after five. Why don't I put together some sandwiches for us?"

"I—I'll help you," Leenie offered. "God knows I need something to do. I'm on the verge of losing my mind."

"Do you need anything from the store?" Kate asked. "If you do, I'll give Frank a call on his cell phone and tell him to—"

"Is Frank not back yet?" Leenie asked.

"Not yet," Kate told her.

"Then please call him. I'd like to speak to him." Leenie motioned for Kate to come with her into the kitchen.

"You two go ahead," Moran said. "I should check in with headquarters."

Once they were in the kitchen, Kate dialed Frank's cell number. He answered on the first ring.

"Latimer."

"Frank, it's Kate."

"What's up? Anything wrong?"

"Nothing new. But Leenie wants to talk to you."

"She does?"

"Yes, she does." Kate held out the phone to Leenie.

She grasped the phone, inhaled and exhaled then said, "Kate and I are going to make sandwiches for supper. They should be ready in about fifteen minutes. Would you please come home and eat with us. Afterward, I want to show you Andrew's photo album and if you'd like to know more about him, I want to tell you about your son."

Kate turned her head and willed herself not to cry. It had been ages since she'd shed a tear. At one time she had thought she'd cried herself dry, that there were no more tears left in her. But every once in a while something happened—usually a case involving a kidnapped child—that stirred long dead emotions within her. Years ago when she'd been a rookie cop on the Atlanta P.D., she'd worked with Ellen Denby and marveled at how the woman could keep a cool head and deal with the toughest cases involving children. But as the years went by and she and Ellen had exchanged confidences, she had learned that they shared a similarly tragic experience which enabled them to understand each other in a way no one else could. Just as Kate understood Leenie as only a mother who'd also had a child stolen from her could understand.

Kate offered to clear up the dishes and surprisingly Moran stayed in the kitchen to help her. Leenie felt as if she'd made a new friend in Kate and understood on an unspoken level that perhaps Kate had suffered once just as she suffered now. She realized she could be wrong about Kate, but her feminine intuition—her gut instincts—told her she was right. Sometime in her past, Kate Malone had lost a child.

Frank had been awfully quiet while they ate sandwiches, chips and cheesecake. She couldn't remember the last time she'd eaten cheesecake twice in one day. Oh yes she did remember—it had been the last time she'd made love with Frank. They'd had cheesecake for breakfast and again for lunch.

Alone together in the living room, Frank and she sat side by side on the sofa while she opened Andrew's baby book, filled with photographs and memorabilia from her pregnancy and Andrew's first two months of life. When Frank made no effort to close the gap between their bodies—the two feet that separated them—she took the initiative and scooted up next to him, hip-to-hip. He flinched, then stiffened. What was wrong with him? She wasn't going to attack him, for pity's sake. She laid the book in her lap and flipped it open so the other side dropped down on his thigh.

"Here's a picture of me at my baby shower," Leenie said. "Elsa came back to Maysville to help Haley host the event."

Frank glanced at the picture, but said nothing.

"I was big as a barrel there. I gained thirty pounds."

"Elsa and Rafe knew you were pregnant?"

"Yes, they knew. And before you get all huffy at Rafe, Elsa threatened him with divorce if he called and told you. She tried to talk me into getting in touch with you, but once she realized she couldn't persuade me, she promised me that neither she nor Rafe would call you because it wasn't their place to tell you."

"You're right. It was your place."

"I thought we'd already agreed that I made a mistake in not informing you I was pregnant with your child. Do we have to continue beating a dead horse?"

Frank glanced at the photo again. "You look happy."

"I was happy." She tried to smile. "Fat and happy."

"You were beautiful pregnant. Fat and beautiful." He grinned, but didn't make eye contact.

"I got even fatter," she told him. "I was only

seven and a half months in that picture.'' She flipped through the pages, slowing on each page long enough for him to glance at it. When she reached the page with Andrew's birth announcement and the first photo of him taken at the hospital, Frank clamped the page open with his big hand.

''Were you alone when he was born or did—''

''Haley was with me.''

''I should have been with you.''

''Yes. And it's my fault you weren't.''

''No, it was only partly your fault. And it was partly my own damn fault.''

''Well, at least we can agree on something—that there's enough blame to share.''

When Leenie heard a phone ring, she tensed. It had to be either Kate's or Moran's cell phone since the ringing came from the kitchen and it wasn't her private line.

''It's not necessarily bad news,'' Frank told her.

''I know. It's just that I—''

The kitchen door swung open; Kate walked in and looked right at Frank. ''Moran wants to see you in the kitchen for a minute.''

''What's wrong?'' Leenie asked. ''And don't tell me it's nothing. I can sense something has happened.''

''You're right,'' Kate admitted, then called into the kitchen. ''We're telling them both, Moran. Leenie needs to know, too. Right now.''

Oh, God, what was it? What had happened?

Moran came out of the kitchen and stood in the open doorway. He glanced from Frank to Leenie, shuffled his feet and said, ''I got a call from Chief Bibb.''

"And?" Frank asked.

Moran hesitated. "They…er…they found a body."

Leenie gasped. Frank put his arm around her waist and held her.

"A baby?" Frank asked.

"Yes. An infant. A boy. Age estimated at one to three months."

"Oh, God, no!" Leenie screamed and suddenly everything went black.

Five

Frank wasn't the type of man easily affected by a woman's tears, swooning spells or temper tantrums. He'd seen it all as a kid—watching his mother, who'd been an expert in feminine wiles, manipulate his father time and again. And he'd learned from that very same father how to harden his heart and shut off his emotions. The only time he'd ever let his defenses down had been with Rita. Bad mistake. Not one he'd repeated. But damn it, catching Leenie in his arms when she fainted dead away had stirred up some unwanted emotions inside him. She wasn't playing him, wasn't putting on an act in an effort to control him. Her actions were real, brought on by true and honest feelings. All he'd wanted to do at that moment was hold and comfort her, protect her from the ugly truth and reassure her that she wasn't alone. And here they were an hour later at the police morgue and still all he wanted to do was protect her, take care of her, shield her from more pain. Already this woman—the mother of his child—had somehow managed to sneak past his defenses and make him vulnerable. He hated feeling vulnerable; it was an alien concept to him.

"You shouldn't have come down here." Chief Bibb cleared his throat as his gaze dropped from Leenie's pale face to the tile floor beneath his feet. "We can get an ID on the body without—"

Leenie gasped quietly. When he felt her stiffen, Frank tightened his grip on her waist. "Andrew's pediatrician or even Haley Wilson could ID the child," Frank said softly. "Why put yourself through this ordeal when it might not even be Andrew?"

"Either way, I have to do this," Leenie said.

Frank studied her, noting the tension in her body and the grave expression on her face.

"No, you don't have to do this." If Frank had been given the chance to know his son, a chance to have been a father from the moment Andrew was born, then he could have come on his own to ID the infant's body. He assumed that in most cases such as this, the father was the one who went to the morgue and put himself through hell in order to protect the child's mother. If only he could do that for Leenie. But he couldn't.

"Yes, Frank, I do have to do this," Leenie told him. "If it isn't Andrew, I need to see that for myself. And if it is…if it is, then I'll know he's dead. I won't spend the rest of my life wondering."

"But if it is Andrew, you'll never be able to forget—"

Kate laid her hand on Frank's back. "Don't try to stop her. She has to do this." Kate reached over and patted Leenie's arm. "I understand how you feel. It's worse not knowing one way or the other, holding on to hope when everyone tells you there is none, than it is having to face the certainty of your child's death."

Leenie clenched her teeth tightly, barely containing her overwrought emotions, then nodded agreement to Kate's comment.

"We're ready," Frank told the coroner, a bald, middle-aged doctor named Huggins.

Securing his arm around her waist, Frank walked with Leenie into the cold, dimly lit room. Dr. Huggins, who had preceded them, walked over to the steel table where a white sheet covered the tiny body. Silence permeated every square inch of the area. Frank heard only his own breathing moments before Leenie sighed aloud. He tightened his grip on her hand. She looked at him, fear and uncertainty in her eyes.

"We'll do this together," he told her.

She nodded.

"All right," Frank said to Dr. Huggins.

The coroner removed the sheet, revealing the small, lifeless body. Frank wanted to pull Leenie back, to rush her out of the room and away from the possible heartache facing her. But she forged ahead, then stopped abruptly to gaze down at the infant's discolored corpse.

Leenie's hand flew to her mouth as she gasped loudly. "Oh, God. God!"

Frank's heart lurched to his throat. His pulse accelerated. *No, please, no,* he prayed silently, the plea a gut-level reaction. But he couldn't bring himself to look at the infant.

Leenie gasped for air. "It's not him. It's not Andrew."

Frank had never known such overwhelming relief. It was then—in that unparalleled moment of thankfulness—that he experienced a personal epiphany. Without ever having seen or held his child, he knew he loved Andrew. And he wanted a chance to be a father to his son.

Kate uttered a loud, gasping sigh. Frank blew out a deep breath. Leenie turned to Frank, a bittersweet smile on her face, and flung herself into his open arms. He held her, stroking her back, comforting her, as she clung to him for dear life. She wept. Only for a few moments. Quietly. But her body trembled uncontrollably long after she stopped crying.

Finally Frank managed to turn her around and head her toward the door. "Let's go home."

She allowed him to escort her from the room and into the outer office where Chief Bibb and Special Agent Moran waited.

"I'll get the car and bring it around to the front door," Kate said as she hurried away.

No one said another word as Frank led Leenie across the room. When they reached the door, she paused and spoke softly to the police chief. "Ryan, when you find out the child's identity, would you please let us know. I—I want to send my condolences to the family."

As long as she lived, she would never forget the image of that tiny infant lying on the cold, steel table. Somewhere out there another mother had lost a child. The only difference between that woman and Leenie was that this other woman had no hope. Her baby boy was dead.

Frank probably didn't understand why she'd pulled away from him the moment they returned to her house or why she'd hurried into the bathroom and locked the door. He had called to her several times, asking her if she was all right and if there was anything he could do for her. But she hadn't responded. Wouldn't. Couldn't. As much as she needed Frank, as desperately as she wanted him close, she had to be alone right now. Alone to cry. Alone to die a thousand deaths in her heart and soul. Alone to work through the wild, mixed emotions she could barely control.

Even before the unknown infant's body had been found, Leenie had felt as if she were on the verge of losing her mind. Although Frank and Kate and Haley had forced her to go through the motions of living, she really didn't feel alive. She felt numb one minute and on fire with terror the next. She wanted to crawl into a hole and die. And at the same time she wanted to run and scream and beat her fists against the wall. It was as if she were dead and alive. Numb and oversensitive. Subdued and crazed. All simultaneously.

After closing the lid, Leenie sat down on the commode and crossed her arms over her chest. She sat there and cried. Soft sobs. A steady stream of tears cascaded down her face. There was an ache inside her that hurt so bad she could barely breathe.

"Oh, Andrew…Andrew."

Frank lifted his hand to knock on the bathroom door again. He'd knocked several times half an hour ago and pleaded with Leenie to answer him, to let him help her. But when she hadn't responded, he'd finally left her alone. He had talked to Kate for a few minutes, then spent the past twenty minutes alone in his son's nursery. He had run his fingers over the hand-painted mural on the wall—a Noah's Ark scene. The walls were a pale blue, the ceiling covered with fluffy clouds and a host of stuffed animals and infant toys lined the floor-to-ceiling shelves. A magic room for a much-loved baby boy.

"Leave her alone." Kate stood in the doorway to Leenie's bedroom.

Frank whirled around to face Kate. "What?"

"Leave Leenie alone. She'll come out when she's ready. You'll have plenty of time to comfort her then, when she needs you. Right now, she needs to hide away."

He didn't know Kate all that well, but had heard the speculations about her that abounded around the Dundee office. "What makes you the expert?" he asked.

"I'm a woman."

"Okay, if being a woman makes you an expert on all things female, then tell me this—why is it that Leenie pulls me to her with one hand and pushes me away with the other? She's blowing hot and cold. I don't know what she wants."

"Believe me, you men are just as big a puzzle to us as we are to you." Kate motioned for him to come toward her. "Let's wait for Leenie in the living room. Eventually she'll come out and that's when you can play knight in shining armor again. Just wait for the signals. A smart man knows when to advance and when to retreat."

"I'm not smart when it comes to women," Frank

admitted, following Kate down the hall and into the living room. "I'm bad at relationships."

They sat down on the sofa. Kate curled up sideways, her waist and lower back supported by the sofa arm. Frank pressed his shoulders into the back of the couch, then crossed one leg over the other knee.

"Your personal life is none of my business. But if you care about Leenie, and I think you do, then ask yourself just how serious you are about a relationship with her. Don't let her believe she can count on you for the long haul if you're just in this until we find Andrew."

Good advice. Hell, great advice. "What if I don't know how I feel or what I want for the future? For now, I want to bring Andrew home. I want to protect Leenie and support her through this ordeal. But..." He shook his head. "I want to be a father to my son."

Kate looked him right in the eye. "But not a husband to your son's mother?"

"You're not one for being subtle, are you?"

"No. I think there's no use beating around the bush. Right? Let's call a spade a spade. You no doubt have your reasons for being afraid of love, of committed relationships. And whatever those reasons are, I don't want or need to know. But Leenie has a right to know why."

"Maybe Leenie doesn't care," Frank said. "You're assuming she wants something permanent with me. Just because we had a child together and right now she needs me doesn't mean she wants a future with me."

"Have you ever thought of just asking her?"

Frank shook his head. "Nope. I've found the direct approach seldom works with women."

Kate made a face, then huffed. "What sort of women have you been dating? Or did one woman do a number on you years ago and now you paint us all with the same brush?"

The truth stung just a tad, but Frank managed to halfway smile at her comment.

Kate opened her mouth, but before she could speak, Frank's cell phone rang. Grateful for the reprieve—he'd figured Kate was about to dish out some more feminine advice or dig deeper into his past personal life—Frank whipped the phone from his pocket and hit the on button.

"Latimer here."

"Yeah, this is Special Agent Moran. We've got a possible break in the Andrew Patton case."

Frank went stiff, his body tense, his breathing momentarily halted. "Have you found him?"

"Sorry, no," Moran replied. "But the abduction ring we've infiltrated is putting up a new infant for adoption. In Tennessee. Memphis to be exact. The baby is male. Blond hair. Blue eyes. Approximately two to three months old. We're making plans now to send in a couple of agents as prospective parents."

"You can't nab the kid right then and there can you?"

"You know we can't. So maybe it's better if you don't share this info with Ms. Patton, unless you're sure she can handle it."

"I'll talk things over with Kate before I decide whether or not to tell Leenie," Frank said. "Keep us posted, will you?"

"Yeah, I will. I know he's your kid and…well… I'll keep you updated."

"Thanks."

Frank understood that these agents, disguised as hopeful, adoptive parents, would simply go in for a first meeting, but wouldn't make any arrests or do anything to alert the top bananas in the abduction ring that the feds were on to them. From what Moran had told Frank, the bureau had been building this case for quite some time, working toward the moment when everything fell together just right. They wanted more than the peons in this dirty business—they wanted the kingpins. The only way to shut down the ring permanently was to destroy it from the top.

After returning his cell phone to his pocket, Frank turned to Kate. "Moran says there's a new infant on the adoption block. Words out from the association the Feds have been investigating that they have a blond-haired, blue-eyed infant ready for adoption."

Kate sucked in her breath. "And they're sending in federal agents posing as a couple desperate to adopt a child, right?"

"Right."

Rubbing the back of his neck, Frank paced around the room. His paternal instincts warred with his logical, trained warrior mind. As a father, he didn't give a damn about anything but rescuing his son. But the Dundee agent in him, as well as the Army Special Forces training that was such a fundamental part of him, acknowledged that the mission outweighed any personal needs. The FBI's mission was not only to return Andrew Patton—unharmed—to his parents, but to destroy a malicious infant adoption ring that had been operating in the Southern states for over a decade.

"She won't understand, will she?" Frank said, his back to Kate.

"No, she won't understand."

"Then I shouldn't tell her. Moran thinks it best not to tell her."

"Moran doesn't have anything personal to lose by not telling Leenie." Kate said. "You do."

"Do I?"

"You tell me."

"I'm willing to bet that once Andrew is back in her arms safe and sound, she'll be willing to forgive me for just about anything."

"Don't count on it. If she ever finds out—"

"If I ever find out what?" Leenie's voice rang out loud and clear from the other side of the room.

Frank snapped around to face her. A wide-eyed Kate glanced from Frank to Leenie and then back to Frank.

"Is it something about Andrew?" Leenie asked, hope in her voice.

Frank grimaced. "Nothing concrete."

"What does that mean?"

Frank looked at Kate, wanting her to say something—anything—to defuse this ticking time bomb before it exploded. One of them had to give Leenie an explanation. Kate looked at him, her expression telling him that she thought it should be him.

Hell, now what was he supposed to do? "It means that the FBI have a lead in the case, but—"

"What sort of lead?" Leenie entered the living room, her face freshly washed, her eyes slightly swollen.

She'd been crying, Frank realized. And now she was approaching him, all but begging him with every look, every move, every word to give her a thread of hope to cling to. "A blue-eyed, blond infant has been put up for adoption in Memphis. His general description fits Andrew—''

"We have to go to Memphis right now," Leenie said emphatically. "Where do they have him? Has Special Agent Moran sent someone to get him? Oh, Frank, this is wonderful news. Andrew is safe and—''

Frank grabbed her by the shoulders. She gasped as her startled gaze met his.

"We don't know that it's Andrew," Frank said.

"But it might be." She offered him a fragile smile. "It has to be."

"We'll know soon enough." He squeezed her shoulders, then eased his hands down her arms, caressing and comforting.

"How soon? Tonight? First thing in the morning? How long do we have to wait?"

"It could be a while." His gut instincts told him that this was not going to go well. Leenie was in no mood to listen to reason. Hell, who could blame her?

She jerked free of his hold and glared at him. "How long is a while? And why do we have to wait? If it's Andrew—and I have to believe that it is—why won't the FBI bring him home to me immediately?''

Frank let out a sigh of relief when Kate injected, "Things are never that simple with the feds. There are procedures to follow, agendas that have to be—''

"No, I don't want you to explain." Leenie held up her hand in a stop signal. "I want Frank to tell me why he isn't moving heaven and earth to get his hands on Andrew and bring him home to me." Narrowing her eyes to slits, she skewered Frank with her angry glare.

Frank cleared his throat, then took a step toward Leenie. Easing backward, she held both hands in front of her, a gesture that warned him not to come any closer.

"Dammit, Slim, don't you think I want that baby to be Andrew? Don't you think I want to drive to Memphis and be the one to go in there and tell those slimeballs that I want to adopt the baby and then get him away from them as quickly as possible?"

"Then why don't you? Why can't we pose as the people wanting to adopt Andrew, then—"

"Moran will send in a couple of federal agents," Frank told her.

Leenie nodded. "All right. And if the baby is Andrew?"

"If these people supposedly representing the birth parents have the baby with them, they're not going to release him immediately to the adoptive couple. A price will have to be agreed on and a second meeting set up to sign legal documents and exchange cash for the infant."

"What are you not telling me?"

Frank swallowed. Damn! She wasn't going to let this go until she knew everything. "It's complicated. The feds have a major case going on, something they've been putting together for quite some time. In order to bring down the ringleaders of the infant abduction ring, they can't do anything that might tip off these people and that includes grabbing this particular infant before the time is right. The entire procedure could take several days, maybe even several weeks."

"I see."

No, she didn't. She didn't see, didn't understand. And she hated him. It was all there in her eyes, in the cold, distant expression.

"Leenie…"

"The FBI has its own agenda and if Andrew gets lost in the shuffle, too bad. He's just one baby out of hundreds, right? What difference does it make if they lose him as long as they save all the others?"

"That's not the way it is." Frank held out his hands to her.

"Yes, it is. You don't have a problem going along with Special Agent Moran's plans, do you? You see the big picture, whereas I see only the little picture. Andrew. My son is all that matters to me. Call me selfish and uncaring of other people's feelings, but all I want is my baby! And if Andrew meant a damn thing to you, he would be all that mattered to you."

"Leenie, give Frank a break," Kate said. "His hands are tied. Moran is in charge and no matter how much Frank and I would like to rush in and grab this baby—be he Andrew or not—we can't. We won't. If we did, we might not only jeopardize the child's life, but we would definitely jeopardize the bureau's operation that is on the verge of—"

"To hell with the bureau's operation. I want my baby! And I'm going to get him." She glowered at Frank. "With or without your help."

Frank glanced at Kate. God help them, Leenie was irrational.

When Leenie ran into her bedroom, Frank turned to Kate. "What do I do now?"

"Be patient and understanding."

"Should I go in there and—"

"No, leave her alone. Let her calm down. I'll check on her in a little while."

Two minutes later Leenie came barreling out of her bedroom. Wearing a black winter coat and carrying her black shoulder bag, she stormed past Kate and Frank on her mad dash to the front door.

"Where are you going?" Frank called to her.

"Where do you think? I'm going to Memphis!"

Frank groaned. Damn it! She'd completely lost it. She wasn't thinking straight. She had no idea where Moran was or where the meeting tomorrow would take place.

"Leenie, come back," he told her when she yanked open the front door.

Ignoring him completely, she rushed outside. Frank ran after her, catching up with her on the sidewalk. When he grabbed her arm, she turned on him, a snarl on her lips and maternal rage shining in her eyes.

"Don't do this," he said. "Slim, pull yourself together. You have no idea where to go in Memphis. And Moran is not going to tell you or me or Kate. Whether we like it or not, all we can do is wait."

"No, dammit, no!" She hurled herself at him, her fists pounding against his chest. "I want my baby. I want Andrew."

He allowed her to vent her anger, frustration and fear by pummeling him repeatedly. When her blows became nothing more than unsteady, weak strikes, he grabbed her and pulled her into his arms. She sank into him. Exhausted. Soul weary. He held her with a fierce protective strength, wanting nothing more in life than to ease her pain.

"We'll get him back," Frank said.

Burrowing against him, her head on his shoulder, she clung to him. And after several minutes, she lifted her head just enough to gaze into his eyes. He hadn't realized he'd gotten emotional until she reached up, caressed the side of his face and then wiped away a lone tear from his cheek.

Six

Making love should always be this wonderful, this intense. Every fiber of her being felt Frank's touch. What had begun with soft gentleness quickly progressed to ravaging hunger. She needed him—wanted him—as a woman wants only that one special man. For her, Frank Latimer was that man.

His mouth was hot and demanding. His tongue probed, then plunged. The kiss consumed her, possessed her. Her body surrendered to the pleasure, reveling in the luscious abandonment. How long had she waited to be with him again? It seemed like forever. Frank was special, different from any other man she'd ever known. They fit together so perfectly and had from the first time they'd made love, as if they were old lovers who had long ago memorized every inch of each other's bodies. He had touched her physically and emotionally on a level she'd never experienced.

He rose up and over her, his big naked body magnificent, his erection projecting outward boldly. As he settled between her thighs, she caressed his sex. He shuddered. She smiled, loving the power she possessed to arouse him unbearably. He allowed her to pet him for a few moments, then eased out of her grasp and probed her body, seeking entrance. Opening herself up to his invasion, she cried out when he entered her, the sensation so satisfying. She loved the feel of him inside her. Big. Hard. Hot.

She looked up at him. He tossed back his head and closed his eyes. Instinctively she lifted herself and wrapped her legs around his hips, bringing him deeper inside her, increasing his pleasure and hers. He groaned. She sighed.

"I can't get enough of you, Slim." He whispered the words as he nuzzled her ear.

"I know the feeling." She kissed his neck.

He withdrew, then plunged deep and hard, burying himself completely inside her. He alternated deep thrusts with heated kisses and damp, demanding forays to her breasts. She tingled from inside out, on fire for him. The tension inside her built gradually, increasing with each earthy, erotic word he spoke. His grunts and moans mingled with an occasional, barely discernable graphic phrase. He told her what he wanted and what he was going to do to her. She responded with incoherent mumbles and escalating desire.

The urges inside her grew in intensity. *Not yet, I want it to last longer,* a part of her begged, while another part of her demanded, *Now, damn it, now. It's too good to wait.*

What was that ringing noise? she wondered. And

where was it coming from? Hadn't she unplugged the phone in her bedroom as she usually did when she and Frank were together? Go away, she wanted to scream. Leave us alone. We've waited such a long time to be together again.

The ringing continued.

Leenie's eyelids popped open. She groaned when she realized she'd been asleep and only dreaming of being with Frank. It had seemed so real, so breath-takingly real.

Suddenly the telephone stopped ringing. Groggy, her mouth dry as cotton, her head filled with cobwebs, she forced herself into a sitting position. She still wore the clothes she'd had on the evening before, including her shoes.

What time was it? How long had she been asleep? Leenie glanced at the lighted digital clock on the bed-side table—7:40 a.m.

As she slid her feet off the bed and onto the floor, yesterday's events flooded her memory. She and Frank had argued about rescuing Andrew. She had been damned and determined to go to Memphis, to-tally irrational, uncaring that she wouldn't have known where to go once she arrived there.

She had taken her frustration and rage out on Frank. She had actually hit him. Repeatedly. And he'd just stood there and let her vent, let her pound his chest with her fists. How could she have done such a thing? She'd never been a violent person.

Oh, Frank, I'm sorry. I'm so sorry.

She vaguely remembered him lifting her up into his arms and carrying her back into the house and... What had happened next? He had laid her on this bed, then Kate had sat with her, talking softly, assuring her that everything possible would be done to bring Andrew home. And then someone gave her an injection? Who? Had Frank called a doctor? Why couldn't she remember clearly?

An insistent rapping on the closed door drew Leenie's attention. "Yes?"

"May I come in?" Kate Malone asked.

"Yes, please." She needed to ask Kate some questions and find out what had happened to her yesterday evening.

Looking like morning sunshine in her brown dress slacks and gold sweater set, her long blond hair neatly restrained in a loose bun at her neck, Kate entered the bedroom. "How are you feeling this morning?"

"Like I've been drugged."

"You were."

Leenie lifted a questioning eyebrow.

Kate smiled. "Forgive us?"

"What are you asking forgiveness for?" Leenie asked.

"You were hysterical, then emotionally wiped out. We couldn't get you to stop crying, so Frank and I agreed that you needed a doctor. We phoned Haley Wilson and she arranged for her physician to make a house call."

"It was Haley's doctor who came to the house? I guess that's the reason I didn't recognize him."

"She tried your doctor first, but he was out of town."

"What did Haley's doctor give me—an elephant tranquilizer?"

Kate chuckled. "Are you that hungover?"

Leenie rubbed either side of her forehead with her

fingertips. "I feel as if I've been run down by a Mack truck."

"Despite that fact, are we forgiven?"

Somehow Leenie managed to get up. When Kate came toward her, she nodded. "You're forgiven. And I'm okay. I don't need any help. However, I do need a shower." She glanced down at herself. "And I need a change of clothes."

"We thought it best to just let you—"

"We? You and Haley? Or you and Frank?"

"All three of us."

"Where is Frank?"

"That was him on the phone. I tried to get to it before the ringing woke you, but—"

"Frank isn't here?"

"No, he left last night, as soon as you went off to sleep."

"I guess I can't blame him for leaving. I said some terrible things to him."

Kate reached out and took Leenie's hands in hers. "He didn't leave because of anything you said or did. And he's coming back later today. He went to Memphis."

Had she heard Kate right? "Frank went to Memphis?"

"He phoned Moran last night and asked if he promised to stay out of the way, could he just be there in town, at FBI headquarters, and wait around for word on Andrew."

Emotion tightened Leenie's throat. She had accused Frank of not caring about Andrew. But he did care, didn't he? Why else would he have gone to Memphis.

"Do you know what time the meeting is today?" Leenie asked.

"The agents are set to go in posing as adoptive parents at ten o'clock."

Leenie pulled her hands from Kate's and hugged herself, determined not to fall apart again. "Why did Frank call? Is there a problem?"

"He called to check on you," Kate said. "When he left here last night, he was worried sick about you."

"Was he?"

"Yes, he was. You've got to know that despite the emotional barrier Frank has erected to keep the world at bay, that man cares about you. It's so obvious to anyone watching him when he's around you that he's in love."

"Kate Malone, I do believe you're a romantic. Otherwise you'd never think Frank was in love with me. I doubt he's capable of falling in love."

"He is. He just doesn't know it yet." Kate looked Leenie square in the eyes. "You're in love with him, aren't you?"

Leenie sighed.

"I know it's none of my business, but—"

"Yes, I'm in love with the big lug. I'm so in love with him that it hurts."

Kate smiled. "Why don't you take a shower while I fix us some breakfast?"

"Sounds like a plan to me."

Kate turned and headed for the door, then paused, glanced over her shoulder and said, "Frank will call us as soon as he knows anything. If the agents get to see the baby, they should be able to tell if it's Andrew or not from all the photos the feds have of him."

"Even if they can't take him away from those horrible people today, I pray that it is Andrew. At least
then, I'll know he's safe."

Frank held his breath, a heartfelt plea repeating in
his head, when Special Agents Currie and Rushing
returned to the field office on Humphreys Blvd. He
waited impatiently while Moran spoke privately to the
two agents who had posed as potential adoptive parents. Despite all his training and the lifelong habit of
employing logic before emotion, right about now
Frank was thinking like a father. A father whose son
had been kidnapped.

The office door opened and Moran came out alone
to meet Frank. Please, God, please, let that baby be
Andrew.

"Sorry it took so long," Moran said.

"Is he or isn't he Andrew?"

Moran shook his head. "No."

Frank felt as if he'd been sucker punched.

"The baby Rushing and Currie was shown is six
months old, has reddish blond hair and has a small
birthmark on his right arm," Moran explained. "Definitely not Andrew Patton."

"Which means Andrew is still out there, his fate
unknown. He might not have been kidnapped by this
abduction ring y'all are investigating."

"Just because this baby wasn't your son doesn't
mean he won't come up on the auction block in a few
days or few weeks."

"I'm not sure his mother can hold it together for
a few more days, let alone a few more weeks."

"Dr. Patton seems like an amazingly strong woman
to me," Moran said.

"Even the strongest person can break under the kind of pressure Leenie is living with on a daily basis. That baby—our baby—means everything to her. If I can't give her some kind of hope that I'll be able to bring him home to her…"

Moran nodded, then glanced down at the floor. "Yeah. Well…yeah."

Uncomfortable discussing such an emotionally personal issue, Frank changed the subject. "How much time before this operation comes to a head?"

"That's confidential info."

"I don't want specifics. No date, time, place. Just a general idea. I think I've got clearance for that much, don't you?"

"A week. Ten days tops. But possibly sooner."

"How soon?"

"A few days."

Frank drew in a deep breath and released it slowly. "Once the operation's in motion, would you let me know? Just in case Andrew is caught up in things."

"Are you sure you want to know before it's all over and done with?"

"I probably don't want to know, but I'd appreciate a call beforehand anyway." What Frank didn't say, but suspected Moran knew anyway was that he needed time to prepare himself in order to be strong for Leenie if the worst happened.

Moran clamped his hand down on Frank's shoulder. "There's always a chance we'll find Andrew. Tell her that. Give her that much hope."

"False hope?" Frank asked.

"I honestly don't know."

Somehow knowing it was Frank, Leenie grabbed the telephone when it rang at two-thirty that after-

noon. Her hand trembled as she placed the receiver to her ear.

"Hello." Her voice quivered.

"Leenie..."

"I've been waiting for your call."

"I know and I'm sorry I didn't call sooner. I'm on the road, heading back to Maysville. I should be there soon."

She knew the news was bad; if it had been good, he'd have already told her. "The baby wasn't Andrew, was he?"

"No, honey, it wasn't Andrew. I'm sorry."

"Me, too." She swallowed. Tears welled up inside her, but did not surface. She was all cried out.

"Moran said that there's a good chance another baby will come up for adoption soon. Maybe in a few days. The next one could be Andrew."

"Yes, it could be."

"Please don't give up hope."

She closed her eyes and willed herself to remain totally in control. Crying wouldn't change anything. Hysterics wouldn't help Andrew. And blaming Frank only hurt them both.

"I won't give up hope," she told him. "You shouldn't either."

"You're right."

"Frank?"

"Huh?"

"Thank you for going to Memphis to be there when... I'm sorry I was so rough on you yesterday. I couldn't see beyond my own hurt to—"

"It's okay, Slim. Honest. I didn't mind being your

whipping boy, if it helped you. God knows I'm not able to do much else to help.''

''That's not true. Your being here helps.''

He didn't respond for several minutes.

''Frank?''

''Yeah, I'm here. Just wishing I was already in Maysville with you. I'd really like to hold you in my arms right now.''

''Me, too. I sure could use a hug.''

''Give me about forty-five minutes and I'll hug the life out of you.''

''Is that a promise?''

''Damn right it is.''

Kate had made herself scarce after telling Leenie she thought she'd go into town for dinner and a movie. ''I need a break, if you think you'll be okay here alone until Frank gets back.'' She hadn't fooled Leenie for a minute. Kate had left so that Leenie and Frank could be alone. But now that she heard Frank's car pulling up in the driveway, Leenie wasn't sure she wanted to be alone with him. She was so needy right now, so desperate to be held and comforted. What if Frank's actions were rooted in his desire to take care of her? She didn't want him being kind to her. She wanted him to love her.

Bracing her shoulders and willing herself to be calm, she opened the front door and waited for him. The moment she saw him, her stomach did a wicked flip-flop and sexual awareness zinged along her nerve endings. Their gazes met and held for an instant and then Frank was there, grabbing her and pulling her into his arms as he walked her backward into the house. Using his foot, he slammed the door shut. He

clutched the back of Leenie's head, his big fingers
spearing into her hair. She gasped half a second before his mouth came down on hers.

He ate at her mouth, his hunger desperately obvious. She wrapped her arms around him and returned
his kiss with equal fury. Rational thought ceased to
exist. For her. And she suspected for him, too. They
wanted each other. Needed each other.

Help me make the world go away was her last co-
herent thought before she tore at the buttons on
Frank's shirt. He released her only long enough to
shrug off his jacket, then he shoved her backward and
onto the sofa. She all but ripped off his shirt and
buttons flew everywhere. They shared kiss after passionate kiss as he yanked her sweater over her head
and hurriedly removed her bra. She gazed up at him
when he came down over her. He blocked out the rest
of the world. Life itself began and ended with Frank
Latimer and with this moment out of time.

When his mouth took hold of her breast to suckle
and tease, Leenie bucked up against him. His hands
dipped under her to lift her hips so that she felt his
pulsating erection pressing into her mound. She slid
her hand between them and cupped his sex.

"I wanted to make slow sweet love to you," he
told her in a hungry, whispered rush of words. "But
I don't know if I can wait."

"I don't want slow and sweet." She rubbed herself
provocatively against him, naked breasts to hairy naked chest. "I need it fast and dirty."

Her slacks landed on the floor, followed quickly by
his. Her panties flew through the air and perched on
a nearby lampshade. His briefs sailed off and onto the
coffee table, atop a copy of *Psychiatry Today*.

His tongue lunged into her mouth just as he hoisted her hips upward to meet his hard, conquering thrust. He hammered into her. She went wild. Blind to everything except Frank. Deaf to everything except the beating of their hearts. Speechless, their only sounds those of grunts and groans and moans of powerful pleasure.

As they went at each other, hot, hungry passion ruling their actions, they toppled off the sofa and onto the floor. Frank rolled her over and placed her on top of him. She rode him at a frenetic pace until she came. Her climax hit her like a tidal wave. Fierce and overwhelming, wiping her out completely. Just as she cried with release, he took the dominant position and with one final stab sent himself over the edge. Growling ferociously, he jetted inside her, not giving a damn that he'd forgotten all about using a condom.

While ripples of the sexual aftermath glided through their bodies, Frank and Leenie lay in the living room floor and held each other. Naked, sated, tension drained from their bodies, he touched her tenderly as she caressed him. Those unbearably sweet moments after the loving prolonged their escape from harsh reality.

Leenie cuddled close. Frank cocooned her in his big, strong arms. She felt safe and protected. And loved.

Please, God, even if he doesn't love me, let me hold on to that hope for a little while, just as I'm clinging to the precious hope that You will keep Andrew safe.

Frank kissed her temple. "Should we talk?"

"No. Not now. Later."

He stood, then held out his hand to her. She rose to her feet and together they gathered up their scattered clothing and walked arm-in-arm into Leenie's bedroom.

"How long did Kate say she'd be gone?" Frank asked.

"Long enough for an early dinner and a movie."

He tossed his clothes on a nearby chair. She did the same.

Frank led her to the bed. She went with him willingly.

She needed Frank as she'd never needed him before, as she'd never needed another human being. Only he could share her every thought, her every feeling. He offered her solace and sweet moments of forgetfulness. Apart, their fears and worries were more than either could bear. But together, holding on to each other for dear life, they could manage to survive a few more hours...a few more days.

Seven

Leenie awakened early the next morning and for a few seconds remembered nothing except the pleasure she had experienced with Frank. He hadn't stayed the night in her bed. After they'd made love for a second time, they had showered together, fixed sandwiches together and talked about Andrew. Being able to share this horrific experience with Andrew's father somehow comforted her in a way she had never dreamed it could. Although there had been no promises exchanged, no words of love spoken between them, Leenie truly believed that Frank cared about her. And about Andrew. Perhaps Kate had been right. Was it possible that Frank loved her and just didn't know it?

After slipping into her thick velour robe, Leenie ventured into the hallway. Silence permeated the house at this early hour. Perhaps Kate and Frank were both still asleep, after all it was only half past five and still dark outside. Wintertime dark. As she made her way into the kitchen, a chill racked her body. Was it a sense of foreboding or simply the chilliness of the house? She'd turn up the thermostat after she set the coffeemaker.

If only Frank had stayed in bed with her all night. Even without sex, it would have been such a comfort to have him within arm's reach, to have been able to reach out and feel his strong presence beside her. How many times had she longed for him during her pregnancy?

Expecting the kitchen to be empty, Leenie gasped when she opened the door and found Frank sitting at the table reading the morning newspaper and drinking a cup of coffee.

"Morning." He glanced up at her and smiled.

She returned his smile, even if it was somewhat tentative and uncertain. "Good morning." She had no idea what last night had meant to him. Had it been nothing more than sex? Just a way to relieve the unbearable tension?

"Sleep well?" he asked.

"Yes, as a matter of fact I did." She looked away from him and toward the coffeemaker on the counter. "Coffee. Wonderful. I could use a shot of caffeine."

When Frank didn't respond, she walked past him, lifted a mug from the mug rack and poured a cup of black coffee. "Is Kate still asleep?" she asked, her back to Frank.

"As far as I know. She's still in her room." Frank set his coffee mug on the table.

"She stayed out pretty late last night, didn't she?

She probably didn't get to sleep until well past eleven.''

"Closer to midnight," Frank said. "She and I stayed up for a while and talked about things."

"About Andrew?"

"About the feds' case involving the infant abduction ring. Kate is more than just a little interested in it, maybe even a little obsessed. I've never seen her quite so involved in a Dundee assignment. She's taking your situation personally, almost as if—"

"As if she understands what it's like to have a child kidnapped?"

Frank closed the newspaper, folded it in half and laid it aside, then looked at Leenie as she pulled out a chair and sat across from him. "Kate is a complex lady. She's warm and friendly, but she never allows anyone to get too close." Frank chuckled. "I can't fault her on that, can I?"

"Maybe her relating to my predicament is nothing more than her having an empathic heart. She seems like a very kind person. I liked her when we first met last winter." Leenie took a sip of coffee, then placed her mug on the table. "Tell me, Frank, why is it that you won't allow anyone to get too close to you? I know your marriage ended in divorce, but—"

"I made a fool of myself over Rita."

A surge of uncontrollable jealousy rose up inside Leenie. She hated Rita, sight unseen. "So Rita hurt you so badly that you decided to never risk being hurt again."

"You make it sound melodramatic. It wasn't. Just an old familiar tale. I cared more for her than she did for me. She found someone she liked better. Or should I say she met someone whose money she liked better.''

''You loved her madly, of course.''

''Of course.''

Hearing him admit it so freely stung Leenie terribly, as if he'd stabbed her in the heart with a very sharp knife. ''Do you still?''

''Do I still what?''

''Love Rita.''

''Good God, no.''

''But you let what she did to you affect every aspect of your life,'' Leenie said. ''Even if you don't love her now, she certainly still has a tremendous influence in your life, doesn't she?''

Frank glared at Leenie, tension etching the lines around his eyes and across his forehead. ''Look, Slim, don't try to psychoanalyze me. And don't try to change me. I am what I am. Yeah, in part that's thanks to Rita. And in part thanks to my mother, who was quite a bit like Rita as a matter of fact. And part of who I am is thanks to my own survival instincts. A guy who makes the same mistake twice is a fool.''

''And Frank Latimer is nobody's fool.''

Their gazes collided, exploded, then when the metaphorical smoke cleared, he looked down at the newspaper and tapped it with his index finger. ''It's going to rain today. We might even get a little sleet.''

''Kate knows there's something between us,'' Leenie said. ''That's why she left us alone yesterday evening…why she stayed gone so long. You could have spent the night in my bed and she wouldn't have been surprised.''

''If you're trying to say something, just say it.''

Not making eye contact with her, he picked up his mug, stood and went to the coffeemaker for a refill.

"Why didn't you stay with me, Frank? We made love. Twice. It's obvious that you care about me, that you care about our son. What are you so afraid of? Did you think sleeping with me all night would have been some sort of commitment, that I'd take it the wrong way and believe there was more to our relationship than there is?"

Full coffee mug in hand, he turned to face her, a somber expression on his face. "What do you want me to say?"

"Just tell me the truth. I think I deserve that much, don't I?"

"The truth is—yeah, I care about you. I did last winter. I do now. The last thing I want to do is hurt you and if I allow you to believe we have a future together... I want to be good to you. I want to help you through this ordeal. I want to bring Andrew home to you. And I want a chance to get to know my son."

Leenie sucked in a deep breath. Even without him saying it, she knew Frank already loved Andrew.

"When Andrew comes home, and he will, you and I will work out an arrangement so that you can be a part of his life." Her pride in need of bolstering and not wanting Frank to suspect that he'd just broken her heart—again—Leenie forced a smile. "And don't think that if we have sex again or even if we sleep all night together some night that I'll start hearing wedding bells and ordering a picket fence to put up around this place. Heck, Frank, I'm the quintessential free spirit who has lost count of the men I've been with over the years. I don't want to be tied down to one man any more than you want to get trapped by some woman.''

God would get her for those lies, Leenie told herself, all the while managing to keep her phony smile in place. She certainly wasn't a simpering virgin, but she was hardly a good-time girl either. She remembered the names of her former lovers because there actually hadn't been all that many and each time she'd been in a relationship, she had hoped he would be ''the one.'' But the biggest lie of all was that she didn't want marriage. She did. Now more than ever. And not marriage to just anyone. She wanted Frank.

He narrowed his gaze as he studied her closely, as if trying to gauge the truth of her declaration. ''Let me give you a little advice about men, Slim. A guy never likes to hear about a woman's former lovers. And he especially doesn't like to hear that there have been so many she can't remember their names.''

Leenie laughed spontaneously. Frank was jealous. But he had no idea that he was. Why would a man be jealous of other men in a woman's life unless he loved that woman? ''Thanks for the advice. I'll remember not to mention my former lovers to my next boyfriend.''

Frank growled quietly, then cleared his throat.

He was so jealous! It was apparent that he hated the idea of her being with another man. Past. Present. Or future.

Don't do this to yourself, Leenie's inner voice cautioned. *Even if Frank does love you, he may never be able to admit it to himself, let alone to you.*

Coming to an understanding, of sorts, they relaxed around each other. The tension between Frank and her should have eased up, and it had—to a certain extent. Beneath the calm alliance binding them together as Andrew's parents lay an ever smoldering sexual edginess. Neither could escape a basic truth—they were in lust, if not in love. And lust was a potent motivator, not as enduring as love, but equally as powerful.

The hours passed slowly, turning the day into night and into day again. During the daylight hours, Kate and Frank kept Leenie busy and occasionally, for brief periods of time, she became so absorbed in whatever she was doing that the ache in her heart diminished a fraction. Those were moments when her entire focus was not on Andrew. But those moments were few and far between. The nighttime hours were the worst, when she lay alone in her bed, longing to hold her baby in her arms. And needing Frank at her side. It had been two days and nights since they'd made love and although he was tender and caring, he had not come to her again.

Leenie kept telling herself that he was afraid of her, of the way she made him feel. He didn't want to love her, didn't want a future with her, but the passion between them was something he could not ignore.

The waiting was wearing on her nerves. How much longer could she hold it together without falling completely apart again? Special Agent Dante Moran had called and talked to her. He'd told her to be patient, to keep hoping for the best, that it could well be only a matter of time before Andrew surfaced as an adoptive infant. So she clung to that hope because it might well be the only hope she had. If her baby had been taken by some woman wanting a child, she might never see him again. And if some lunatic had kidnapped Andrew, her baby was probably already dead.

Leenie shook her head, an effort to dislodge all morbid thoughts. Andrew was alive. He would come home to her. Frank kept repeating those words to her over and over again, as if he was trying desperately to convince himself as well as her.

"Are you ready to go?" Frank asked.

She nodded. "Yes, I'm ready."

The first thing on the keep-Leenie-busy schedule for today was a visit to the hospital to see Debra, who was now resting comfortably in a private room. The doctors had said Debra might be released in a week or less. She had recovered remarkably well for a woman of sixty.

"Stay as long as you'd like," Kate told them as they headed for the front door. "As a matter of fact, why don't you two go out for lunch after your visit to Mrs. Schmale. I can hold down the fort here and if I get any news, I'll phone y'all immediately."

"I'd like to run by the station," Leenie said. "Haley suggested that I might want to give a statement about Andrew's abduction and make a personal plea for his return. I simply haven't been up to doing something like that before now. WJMM has been broadcasting Andrew's photograph periodically, with the news about his kidnapping, but Haley thinks a message from me might actually influence his abductor to return him."

"Since Moran has given you the okay to make a public statement, I see no reason why you shouldn't," Frank said.

"Just so long as you don't mention the infant abduction ring," Kate reminded her. "You don't want to do anything that might alert them that the feds are on to them."

Leenie sighed. "God, I hope Andrew was taken by those damn people. It's the one sure chance we have of getting him back, isn't it?"

Frank put his arm around Leenie's shoulders. "Come on, Slim, let's go see Mrs. Schmale, then I'll take you out for lunch. I'm in the mood for…a greasy hamburger and fries. And maybe a chocolate milk-shake."

Leenie smiled. "Just thinking about that kind of food has already put five pounds on me, mostly on my hips."

Frank's arm slipped down her back and encircled her waist. One hand slid down to cup her hip. "Five pounds won't hurt you. Hell, ten pounds wouldn't."

"Frank Latimer, you know just what to say to a girl to make her happy, don't you?"

"I try," he said, sincerity and a touch of sadness in his voice.

Frank liked Debra Schmale and could see why Leenie had hired her as Andrew's nanny. She possessed a kind disposition and maternal love oozed from her pores. The woman's hospital room looked like a florist. Floral arrangements of every size and kind filled the small private room and four balloon bouquets floated in the air, held in place by ribbon streamers tied to both chairs in the room and to the knobs on the closet doors.

Leenie hugged Debra, careful not to squeeze too hard and hurt the healing patient. "It's good to see you looking so well. I've been worried about you."

"I'll be just fine…once we get Andrew back. I feel so guilty for—"

"Hush that kind of talk," Leenie said. "You have nothing to feel guilty about."

"If only I could have stopped that woman from taking Andrew."

"Mrs. Schmale, you had no way of knowing that the woman had deliberately crashed into your car so that she could kidnap Andrew. You did exactly what anyone would have done," Frank told her as he walked over and stood directly behind Leenie.

"Please, call me Debra." She offered him a warm, genuine smile. "I'm so glad that you're here with Leenie. She needs you, now, more than ever."

Leenie gasped softly. Frank realized that Mrs. Schmale—Debra—knew he was Andrew's father, which made him wonder just how much Leenie had told her about him.

"In case you're wondering, Leenie told me very little about you, not even your name," Debra said, as if reading his mind. "She didn't offer the information and I didn't pry.

"Then how did you know—?" Leenie asked.

"Haley told me about Mr. Latimer. She's been a frequent visitor. And she is as pleased as I am that Andrew's father is by your side during this terrible ordeal."

When Debra looked at Frank, she smiled, but he felt her disapproval and understood she was wondering why he had gotten Leenie pregnant and walked out of her life. Women of Debra Schmale's generation expected a man to do the right thing, to make an honest woman of his child's mother.

"You and Haley are a couple of busybodies," Leenie said jokingly. "And just so you won't badger

Frank, you should know that he plans to be a part of Andrew's life...once we have him back with us.''

"There's no news, then?'' Debra asked.

Leenie shook her head.

Frank put his arm around Leenie's waist and pulled her close. "We have every reason to hope that no news is good news, at least for now. The FBI thinks Andrew will be found unharmed. Leenie and I are clinging to that hope.''

Debra eyed Frank's arm around Leenie.

The telephone on Debra's bedside table rang. She reached out for it, but Leenie grabbed it to save Debra the effort.

"I've gotten a dozen calls already today,'' Debra told Frank. "Everyone in Maysville must know I'm out of ICU and in a private room now.''

"Debra Schmale's room,'' Leenie said.

Frank glanced at Leenie, who paled instantly.

Leenie looked at Frank and said, "It's Kate and she wants to speak to you.''

The muscles in Frank's belly knotted painfully. He reached out and took the receiver from Leenie. "Yeah, Kate, what's up?''

"Moran just called,'' Kate said.

"Tell me it's good news.''

Leenie grasped Frank's arm.

"It could be,'' Kate told him. "Two new infants have come up for adoption. Both fit Andrew's description.''

"When is he sending in a couple of agents?'' Frank asked.

"What is it?'' Leenie demanded, tugging on Frank's arm. "Is it news about Andrew?''

"Everything is set up for tomorrow,'' Kate said.

"Moran wanted me to tell you something. He made me repeat it twice."

"What?"

"He said to tell you that it's sooner rather than later."

"God!" The FBI operation that had been in the works for several years was coming together. Sooner rather than later. Possibly tomorrow? Was that what Moran was trying to tell him? Was it all going to happen tomorrow, right when Andrew—if he was one of the two infants—would be smack dab in the middle of everything? What if when the feds made their arrests, the two babies were whisked away before being rescued? What if they lost Andrew? What if there was gunplay?

"I'll bring Leenie home right away," Frank told Kate. "We'll skip going to WJMM today."

"Moran knows you'll come back to Memphis."

"Damn straight about that." Frank replaced the receiver and turned to Leenie, who was squeezing the life out of his arm. "Good news. A couple of infants have been found and it's possible one of them is Andrew." He glanced at Debra Schmale and smiled, then gave Leenie a sharp glare, hoping she'd understand why he couldn't be totally forthcoming with Debra.

"This is wonderful news," Debra said.

"Keep it to yourself for now, okay?" Frank smiled at her.

"Absolutely." Debra folded her hands together in a prayerlike gesture.

"We need to go," Frank told Leenie.

She kissed Debra on the forehead and said her goodbyes, then rushed out of the room with Frank.

When they were alone in the elevator, she didn't wait for him to explain.

"Two more infants have come up for adoption, right?" she asked.

"Right."

"In Memphis?"

"Yeah."

"You're going to Memphis tonight, aren't you?"

"Yeah."

"And you want me to stay here in Maysville and wait."

"Yeah."

The elevator doors swung open and they emerged on the first floor. Frank grabbed her arm and hurried her outside to the parking lot. She walked quickly to keep up with his long-legged gait. When they reached his rental car, she halted and dug in her heels.

Before she could speak, he grabbed her by the shoulders and said, "Dammit, Slim, stay here in Maysville, will you? Let me be the big, strong man. Let me be your man."

"You want to be a buffer between me and the big bad world, don't you?"

"Something like that. After all, I am Andrew's father. I wasn't around when you were pregnant or when you gave birth. I should have been. You needed me and I let you down.

"I need to do this for you. Hell, I need to do it for myself. Let me be the one to handle things, and if it is Andrew, I want to be the one to bring him home to you."

"And if it isn't Andrew?"

"Then I should be the one to tell you. We're Andrew's parents. And if we've lost him, we should share that grief together.''

Leenie swallowed, then offered Frank a fragile smile. Tears gathered in the corners of her eyes. ''You go to Memphis. I'll wait here in Maysville for you...and Andrew.''

He cupped her face with his hands, then kissed her.

Eight

Frank had left for Memphis around eight-thirty last night and called after he arrived at the hotel. Leenie and Kate had sat up until after two this morning, watching television, talking, looking through magazines, listening to Leenie's substitute on WJMM's late-night talk show. They had done anything they could think of to kill time. At midnight, while listening to the radio, they made fudge and devoured a third of what they'd prepared. As if by silent agreement, they hadn't mentioned Frank or Andrew. At two, they'd gone to their separate bedrooms and Leenie had tried her best to sleep. She had tossed and turned for hours. Finally giving up hope of getting any rest, she'd flipped on the bedside lamp and searched for a romance novel in her stash of to-be-read paperbacks. As entertaining as the book was, Leenie simply could not concentrate enough to do the story justice, so around four-thirty, she'd taken a shower and put on jeans and a sweatshirt.

As she passed the floor-to-ceiling mirror in the hallway, she caught a glimpse of her image. She looked bleary-eyed and somber. Her damp hair was secured in a loose ponytail. Faded jeans hugged her hips and legs. A comfy green fleece sweatshirt with an enormous sunflower in the center gave her otherwise pale appearance a touch of color. All-in-all, she was a pitiful sight.

She wondered if Frank had gotten any sleep last night. Probably not. If only she'd gone with him, at least they'd be together right now. But Frank had needed to make the trip to Memphis alone. She understood. And deep in her primitive feminine heart, she loved him all the more for wanting to play the role of her protector.

How was it possible that her whole world had become condensed into one event—into what happened this morning in Memphis, at some immoral, money-hungry lawyer's office? Two FBI agents would once again pose as prospective parents, but would they get to see the two infants who were available for adoption? Would one of those babies be Andrew? If Andrew hadn't been kidnapped in order to sell him to the highest bidder, then she might never know his fate. Could she live that way, never knowing?

When Leenie entered the kitchen, she glanced at the wall clock. Five-fifteen. The meeting was set for nine o'clock this morning. Less than four hours from now. But how long would it take the agents to report back to Moran if they did get to see the babies? It was possible that even after the meeting, they still wouldn't know if Andrew was one of the two infants.

While preparing the coffee machine, she stared at the telephone. She wanted to talk to Frank, to hear his voice. But he might be asleep. She shouldn't disturb him.

She reached out and jerked the receiver from the wall phone, then glanced at Frank's cell number, which he'd jotted down on the bulletin board by the telephone. After dialing, she suddenly had second thoughts and started to hang up, but Frank answered on the second ring.

"Latimer here."

"Frank?"

"Leenie? Honey, are you all right?"

"I'm okay. I didn't sleep much."

"You didn't sleep at all, did you?"

"No, I didn't," she admitted. "I'll bet you didn't either."

"I closed my eyes a few times, but... We'll both sleep once I bring Andrew home."

"I—I want you to know that if neither baby is Andrew—" Emotion tightened her throat. She swallowed. "It won't be your fault, so don't blame yourself."

"We can't lose hope, even if neither baby is Andrew. He's out there somewhere. We'll keep searching."

"I'm going to hang up now." Her voice quivered. "Before I start blubbering."

"Yeah, we don't want that, do we? If you start, I might, too. And that would blow my macho image to hell and back."

"Nothing could destroy your macho image, least of all crying for your lost son."

"Leenie...I...keep praying, will you?"

"Mmm-hmm."

"I'll call you as soon as I know anything."

"Yes…please…"

"Bye, Slim."

"Bye."

With the dial tone humming in her ear, Leenie stood there and forced back the tears that ached inside her. These next few hours were going to be the longest of her life.

By the time Leenie downed her second cup of coffee and was munching on a slice of buttered toast, Kate entered the kitchen. Wearing a pair of flame-red sweats, her hair hanging loosely around her shoulders, Kate looked like a teenager, all fresh-faced and glowing with good health.

"How long have you been up?" Kate asked, as she headed for the coffeepot. "Or should I say how long have you been in the kitchen? I figure you've been up most of the night."

"I came in the kitchen about forty-five minutes ago."

"Hmm-mmm." Kate poured herself a cup of coffee, then sat across from Leenie.

"I called Frank."

Kate raised an inquisitive eyebrow.

"He's going to call back the minute he knows something," Leenie said.

Kate took a sip of coffee, clutched the mug with both hands and looked right at Leenie.

"I hope and pray one of those baby boys is Andrew. But while you're hoping for the best, you have to prepare yourself for the worst."

"I don't know if I can do that. I don't want to think about what it'll mean if—"

"It doesn't mean you have to give up hope. As long as you don't have proof that Andrew is dead, then no one can take your hope away from you," Kate said emphatically.

Leenie stared at Kate, puzzled by the fierceness in her voice, by the resolute certainty of her statement. "What is it that you still hope for, Kate?"

Gripping the mug she held as if it were her anchor in a stormy sea, Kate closed her eyes for a split second, then opened them and looked directly at Leenie again. "I hope that out there somewhere, my little girl is alive and well and somebody is loving her and taking good care of her."

Rendered speechless by Kate's honesty, Leenie gaped soundlessly, her heartbeat drumming in her ears. Although she had suspected Kate had lost a child, hearing her admit it tore at Leenie's heart. "Was your child...your daughter kidnapped?"

"Yes. Mary Kate was barely two months old when it happened."

Kate inhaled and exhaled slowly. Leenie figured the deep breathing technique was a tool Kate used to keep her emotions in check. Despite her in-control-at-all-times facade, Kate occasionally let her vulnerability show. And Leenie liked her all the more for those tiny lapses.

"Mary Kate was kidnapped eleven years ago," Kate said. "At the time, we thought she'd been taken for ransom because my husband—my ex-husband now—is a member of a very wealthy and prominent family."

"But she wasn't taken for ransom?"

Kate shook her head. "The FBI was brought in, of course, and we waited for the call or the letter to tell us how much money the kidnappers wanted. But there was no call. No letter. Trent hired a private firm to search for our daughter, but they never found her, of course. And after a while, Trent convinced himself that Mary Kate was dead.''

''What made him think she was—''

''Nothing in particular. I believe it was the only way he could cope with what had happened. He loved her as much as I did. We just coped with her loss in different ways.'' Kate set the mug on the table and laid her hands flat against the wooden surface on either side of the mug. ''We argued about it day and night. I told him he was wrong to give up hope and he told me I was living in a fantasy world if I thought we'd ever find Mary Kate, that she was dead.''

''It's apparent that you never changed your mind, that you still believe your child is alive. Did your ex-husband ever come around to your way of thinking?''

''No. And that, along with his family's interference and Trent's feelings of guilt and my feelings of guilt…and the endless arguments, destroyed our marriage. We've been divorced ten years now. And I haven't seen him since the divorce became final.''

''But you still love him, don't you?''

Kate laughed, the sound mirthless, stilted. ''Now who's the romantic?''

''You've never remarried, have you? That means something.''

''It means I'm afraid of being hurt,'' Kate admitted. ''Besides, most men want children and I know that I could never have another child and risk losing her or him. The pain is too great.'' Kate gasped. ''Oh, God, Leenie, I'm sorry. I shouldn't have—''

Leenie reached across the table and grasped Kate's

hand in hers. "We haven't lost Andrew. Just as you have somehow managed to keep the faith for eleven years, I'm not giving up hope. Not now, after only a few days. And not ever. If I keep telling myself over and over again that one of those babies the abduction ring is putting up for sale is Andrew, then it will be. It has to be!"

Kate squeezed Leenie's hand. "Yes, it will be."

"And someday you'll find your daughter."

"I believe Mary Kate is alive. If she weren't, I'd know it, wouldn't I? In my mother's heart. Wouldn't you know if— Oh, damn, I keep saying all the wrong things."

"No, you don't," Leenie assured her. "I understand what you mean. But I honestly don't know if my believing Andrew is alive is because I'd know in my heart if he wasn't, or if it's because I simply cannot accept the possibility that…" Leenie paused, her emotions so raw she feared bursting into tears. "I can't even say it."

"Then don't say it. Don't even think it."

"I wouldn't want to live in a world without Andrew." Leenie clenched her teeth tightly, determined not to cry.

Kate squeezed her hand again. They looked at each other, tears misting their eyes, their deepest, darkest fears kept just below the surface.

Frank paced the floor in the Memphis FBI office on Humphreys Blvd. He'd drunk the equivalent of three pots of coffee since he'd arrived this morning and he'd all but worn a hole in the floor. It was nearly three-thirty. Where the hell was Moran? The last word they'd had from the agents involved in the operation was around noon and Frank had been privy to the information only because Moran had personally okayed it. All Frank knew was that the two male infants had been taken into FBI custody and were being checked by a local pediatrician. From overhearing snippets of conversation that the office personnel didn't share with him, Frank had figured out that arrests were being made, the ringleaders of the abduction ring gathered up, along with the lawyers involved in the illegal adoptions.

As much as Frank appreciated the importance of the bureau's great victory in this case, what mattered most to him was finding out if one of those babies was his son. Leenie's son. If only there was some way to find out, if only there was something he could do. But all he could do was wait. And hope. And pray. He'd done more praying these past few days than he'd done all his life. But he supposed when things seemed hopeless was the time a man was most likely to turn to prayer. Frank had known hopelessness before, but not helplessness.

He knew that the feds weren't deliberately keeping any pertinent information about his son from him. During this case, Moran had shared more confidential info than was probably legal and Frank appreciated that fact. And he believed that Moran would let him know something about the babies just as soon as either could be identified as Andrew, or both could be ruled out as his and Leenie's son. The federal agents had regulations and procedures they had to follow and even though Moran had bent a few rules lately, he couldn't give Frank information he didn't have. Not yet. But soon. It was only a matter of waiting on a definite ID for both baby boys.

A flurry of activity occurred outside Moran's office where Frank had been waiting impatiently. Doors slammed, voices rose and suddenly Moran came barreling into his office, a wide smile on his face.

"We got 'em," Moran said. "Every slimy, fat-cat, freaking bastard. We took them down from the top. We arrested twenty people, including the four masterminds and three of their lawyers." He slapped Frank on the back. "By God, it's over. And now we've got ourselves one hell of a mess."

"Where are the babies?" Frank asked. "Is one of them—"

"We've got nearly twelve years of adoption records. Confiscated. Records of children who were probably all abducted from their parents and sold to adoptive families. Do you have any idea what that means? Biological parents and adoptive parents and hundreds of children caught in the middle. It's not only a legal nightmare, but a moral dilemma for everyone involved."

Frank grabbed Moran's shoulder. "Damn it, I'm interested in one child. My son. Where the hell are those babies? Is one of them Andrew?"

"Dr. Tomlin's office hasn't called?" Moran asked as he eased out from under Frank's tenacious grasp.

"Who's—is he the pediatrician in charge of the babies? If so, then no, he hasn't called. Or if he has no one has bothered to tell me."

"The agents who went into this morning's meeting as adoptive parents weren't able to positively ID either child they were shown, but one of the babies fit Andrew's description to a tee." Moran walked over to his desk and picked up the telephone. "I'll make arrangements to take you to Dr. Tomlin's office. Both babies are being kept there for the time being. If one of them is positively identified as Andrew, I'll see to it that you can take him home to his mother this evening.''

"What the hell are you waiting for? Make the call. Now!''

The telephone rang. Kate and Leenie jumped simultaneously. They exchanged quick glances, then Kate shot up off the sofa and grabbed the receiver. Before she could even say hello, Frank spoke.

"I've got him,'' Frank said. "All fourteen pounds of him. Can you hear him squalling. He's not sure whether or not he likes his old man.''

Kate smiled. She'd never heard Frank Latimer enthusiastic about anything, never heard such pure joy in his voice. "Calm down and tell me what's going on.''

"Is it Frank?'' Leenie asked as she came toward Kate.

Kate nodded and mouthed the word yes.

"Look, I've got to change his diaper and I'm not sure I even know how. Just tell Leenie that I'm bringing Andrew home to her tonight. And tell her he's fine.''

"Wait!'' Kate barely had the word out of her mouth when the dial tone buzzed.

"Does he have Andrew?'' Leenie asked.

"He said to tell you that he has Andrew and—''

"Oh, God!'' Leenie grabbed Kate, who still held the telephone in her hand. "Thank you, God.''

Kate eased the phone back on the hook and wrapped her arms around Leenie. "Frank said that

Andrew is fine. He's bringing your son home to you tonight.''

"I wanted to talk to him, to ask him a dozen questions. Why did he hang up so quickly?"

"I believe Andrew needed an immediate diaper change and Frank was feeling a little overwhelmed by the daunting task. I don't think he's ever changed a diaper before."

Leenie's joyous laughter was contagious and within seconds she and Kate were giggling and hugging and dancing around the room like a couple of adolescents. And when they'd exhausted themselves, they fell onto the sofa, all smiles and giddiness.

"I'll never ask for anything again as long as I live," Leenie said. "All my prayers have been answered."

"You're very lucky," Kate told her. "You're getting your son back and I have a feeling it's only a matter of time before Frank realizes that he wants to spend the rest of his life with you and Andrew. You should have heard him on the phone. The guy was delirious with fatherly pride."

Leenie sighed. "Loving Andrew and loving me are two different things. I can't expect Frank to want me on a permanent basis just because he wants to be a father to Andrew."

"Ready for some more unsolicited advice?"

"Sure. Advise away."

"Don't put any pressure on Frank. Let him do things his way, in his own time. When he brings Andrew home, just enjoy the time y'all have together and don't worry too much about the future."

"Kate, I wish…well, I know you must be thinking about Mary Kate and wondering why I'm getting my son back so quickly and your little girl has been missing for eleven years.''

Kate shrugged. ''Life's a mystery. Why I haven't found Mary Kate after over a decade of searching and why your Andrew is being returned to you only days after losing him is one of those mysteries.'' Kate patted Leenie's hand. ''Somehow, someway, someday, I'll find out what happened to my daughter. But for now, for tonight, you just concentrate on celebrating Andrew's return.''

Frank hadn't had a clue that he'd go ga-ga over a two-month-old kid. But the minute Dr. Tomlin's nurse put Andrew in his arms, Frank had melted like ice in the July sun. His little boy had looked at him with Leenie's big blue eyes and he'd been a goner on the spot.

''Is this Andrew Patton?'' Dante Moran had asked, pointing to the child Dr. Tomlin's nurse held.

''We've matched his footprint to Andrew Patton's footprint taken at birth and they're a perfect match,'' Dr. Tomlin had said. ''This young man is definitely Andrew.''

Yes, he certainly was. Andrew. His son. Frank had inspected the kid from top to bottom and seen himself or Leenie in every feature. Odd how he loved the child instantly, and not just because Andrew was his, but because Andrew was Leenie's.

Glancing in the rearview mirror of the rental car he was driving, Frank caught a shadowy glimpse of his son asleep in the carseat Dr. Tomlin had provided. Poor little guy, Frank thought. He'd worn himself out bellowing. Apparently Andrew hadn't inherited Leenie's sunny disposition. Of course, Andrew had been through a traumatic experience, being snatched away from the security of his mother's arms and the loving care of Debra Schmale.

"It's okay, kid," Frank said to the sleeping child, "I'm taking you home to your mama. We should be there in a few minutes. And as for your inheriting my grumpy disposition, don't worry about it. Women seem to go for surly, brooding men."

When Leenie's house came into view, Frank's gut tightened. Because of the bad weather—rain mixed with sleet—he'd driven much slower than his usual speed, so it had taken longer than it should have to make the drive from Memphis to Maysville. But he didn't want to take any chances with Andrew on-board. From now on, his top priority was going to be keeping his son safe. He didn't want Leenie to ever again have to endure the anguish she'd suffered these past few days.

The minute he pulled into the driveway, the front door flew open and Leenie ran outside, off the porch and into the yard. By the time he stopped the car, she was yanking on the back door handle. Frank unlocked the doors, undid his seat belt and got out, but before he could even say hello, Leenie was removing a sleeping Andrew from the carseat. She wrapped him in the blanket she'd brought with her and took him out of the car. She turned to Frank then and smiled as tears streamed down her cheeks. He put his hand on the small of her back and together they hurried into the house. Kate stood just inside the foyer, a warm smile on her face.

Suddenly Andrew let out a loud yowl. Leenie flung the damp blanket to the floor and crushed her baby to her chest. That one yowl turned into a screaming fit. Leenie held him away from her and looked at him, then spoke to him softly, a mother's tender rambling words to soothe her fretful child. Andrew didn't respond immediately, but Leenie kept talking to him and caressing him. Within minutes his crying diminished and soon stopped altogether. He focused his big blue eyes on his mother.

"Hello, my darling," Leenie said, then covered his little face with kisses.

Andrew whimpered, then cooed.

Frank thought he'd lose it right then and there. Hell, he couldn't remember the last time he'd cried. After his father's funeral? Yeah, that had been the last time. When he'd been alone. But seeing his son safe in Leenie's arms was enough to bring a grown man to his knees. She had a magic touch, the ability to soothe Andrew's surly Latimer disposition. Why should that surprise him? Hadn't she been able to work that same magic on him?

"I'm so happy that everything turned out this way," Kate said. "I'm going to make myself scarce so y'all can have this time alone with your son."

Cuddling Andrew close, Leenie said, "No, Kate, you don't have to—"

"This is family time—mother, father and baby time." Kate headed toward the guest bedroom. "I'll see y'all in the morning."

Frank followed Leenie into the living room and sat down beside her on the sofa. He lifted his arm and put it around her shoulders, encompassing her in his embrace as she did Andrew. They sat there together, the three of them, Andrew secure in his mother's arms. Frank couldn't remember ever feeling so good.

"You brought him home to me, just the way you

said you would.'' Leenie kissed the top of Andrew's head. The baby's eyelids drooped.

"He's a beautiful child," Frank told her. "Just perfect. And that's amazing considering I'm his father."

Leenie laughed. And dear God, how strongly her laughter affected him. He'd never heard a sweeter sound.

"Has he been fed? Did you give him a bottle or—"

"I've changed his diaper twice and given him a bottle. Dr. Tomlin, the pediatrician the FBI used in Memphis, gave me three bottles of formula."

"I breast-fed him, you know. I'd just weaned him onto a bottle when the wreck happened and he was taken…" Leenie gulped down a sob.

Frank hugged her closer. "He's home. He's safe. The nightmare is over."

"I don't think I'll ever let him out of my sight again as long as I live."

Frank chuckled. "Yeah, I know the feeling, but I think Andrew will object when you start going out on his dates with him."

"He's not even three months old and you're already talking about him dating."

"Hey, if he takes after his old man, he'll have a girlfriend in kindergarten. Actually, he'll have half a dozen girlfriends."

"I will not allow my son to be a ladies' man." Leenie tore her gaze away from Andrew to look at Frank. "But I won't mind if he takes after you in other ways. You, Frank Latimer, are quite a man and I'm glad you're my son's father."

An embarrassing flush warmed Frank's face. No one had ever told him anything that affected him so strongly. His masculine pride doubled instantly. He leaned over and kissed Leenie, a gentle, fleeting kiss. ''He's the luckiest kid in the world having you for a mother.''

Nine

Frank locked up and set the security alarm after Leenie went to her bedroom, a fast-asleep Andrew cradled in her arms. These past few days had been the longest, most grueling days of his life, and he knew they'd been even worse for Leenie. He loved watching her with Andrew, the way she touched their child, the way the sound of her voice soothed him. For all her sexy, sophisticated, career-woman exterior, Leenie was a mother at heart. Of course, one was not exclusive of the other. He figured Dr. Lurleen Patton was what people might call a multifaceted woman. And he sure as hell had never known anyone like her. She wasn't anything like his mother, who'd never done a selfless thing in her life, who had put her own needs above her son's and daughter's needs time and again. And Leenie bore no resemblance to his former wife. What had he ever seen in Rita, beyond her flashy good looks?

Listen to yourself, Latimer, you sound like a man in love. No way! Even if he did like Leenie, even care about her deeply, he wasn't fool enough to fall in love. Never again. Once had been one time too many. Okay, so Leenie was as different from Rita as night is from day. It didn't matter. Love was no guarantee of happiness. And what could start out as a wonderful relationship—like he'd thought his marriage to Rita was—could turn out to be very wrong. There were too many unknowns between two people. He had seen a lot of promising relationships end up in the gutter, a couple battling it out in the divorce courts. He and Leenie were too smart to make forever promises, to risk not only messing up their lives, but Andrew's too. Wasn't the kid better off with two parents who liked and respected each other and shared the responsibilities of raising him than parents who'd been madly in love and ended up fighting over who was going to get custody of him when they split?

Frank turned out all the lights, except the one lamp in the corner of the living room. He removed his cell phone from his pocket and dialed Sawyer MacNamara's private number. He could easily wait until morning to call his boss, but now that he'd made his decision to keep things friendly but not committed between Leenie and him, he wanted to forge ahead with his plans to become acquainted with his son. He needed some time off, some time to spend with Andrew. And during that time, he and Leenie could figure out how they wanted to handle their joint parenthood. Right now, with Andrew a baby, he probably needed Leenie more than he needed Frank. But as he grew older, he might need Frank more. He could suggest to Leenie that they take things a year at a time and see how things worked out as their son matured.

Sawyer answered his phone on the third ring. ''McNamara here.''

''Yeah, it's Frank Latimer.''

''I spoke to Moran earlier and then to Kate. I'm glad to know everything worked out and you were able to take the baby home to his mother. Kate tells me that the child is well.''

''Andrew is fine, now that he's with his mother.'' Frank paused for a moment, then made his request. ''I need some time off. A week, maybe ten days. Leenie…Dr. Patton and I have some things to work out about Andrew. And I'd like a chance to get to know my son before I head back to Atlanta and go out on another case.''

''A week, even two, can be arranged,'' Sawyer said. ''And if you need more time—''

''Ten days, tops.''

''Good thing I hired Geoff Monday. He can pick up some of the slack and fill in for you and Kate until you're both back on the job.''

''Kate's taking time off, too? Why? I thought she'd be flying back to Atlanta tomorrow.''

''She asked for a leave of absence for personal reasons. I figured she might have told you what those reasons were.''

''She hasn't said a word to me.''

''Okay. So, we'll see you back at the office in a couple of weeks.''

''A week to ten days,'' Frank corrected.

''Fine. A week to ten days. Good luck, Frank. I

hope you and Dr. Patton can come to an amicable agreement about your son.''

"Thanks. I see no reason why we can't. Leenie is a reasonable woman. And being a psychiatrist, she knows how important it is for a child to have two parents who have an amicable relationship.''

"Sounds like you've got it all worked out, at least from your point of view.''

"Yeah. I do.''

After he finished talking to Sawyer, doubts started creeping into his mind. Maybe Leenie wouldn't be cooperative, maybe she wouldn't like the idea of sharing Andrew. After all, she hadn't let him know she was pregnant, hadn't informed him after Andrew was born that he had a son. If Andrew hadn't been kidnapped, would she have ever told him about his child's existence?

Rubbing the back of his neck as he stretched, Frank groaned. He was tired and sleepy. And confused. He needed a good night's sleep. Then in the morning, he'd be able to think straight.

As he walked down the hall, he noticed Leenie's bedroom door stood open. He couldn't resist peeking in on her and Andrew. He stopped in the doorway. His gut clenched when he saw Leenie, in her pink silk gown, lying in bed, her long hair fanned out on her pillow, and Andrew, in his blue terrycloth pajamas, cuddled against Leenie's chest. Mother and child.

His son.

His woman!

Damn, why couldn't he stop thinking of Leenie as his. These past few days he'd become much too possessive of her. How could they build separate lives if he kept laying claim to her?

Face the facts, he told himself. Eventually Leenie was going to start dating again. There would be other men in her life. Other men in Andrew's life, whether he liked it or not. No! He didn't want other men parading in and out of his son's life. But who was to say that Leenie wouldn't find one special guy and get married. It could happen. And then Andrew would have a stepfather.

He had to stop doing this to himself. Don't start making decisions based on what ifs, he told himself.

As he watched Leenie and Andrew sleeping, he was so drawn to them that he couldn't resist the temptation to be near them. It wasn't as if he was invading her privacy. She'd left the door open, hadn't she? She'd probably expected him to check on them before he turned in for the night. Leaving the door open the way she had was an invitation, wasn't it?

Frank walked quietly into the room, not stopping until he reached the bed. What would it hurt if he stayed here with them? Just for tonight. After all, it was Andrew's homecoming. But if he lay down beside them, he might waken Leenie and God knew she needed her rest after all she'd been through. But he could not bring himself to leave. Glancing around the semidark room, he noticed the comfy overstuffed chair in the corner. He could rest comfortably there without disturbing Leenie and Andrew and at the same time, he could be with them, keep watch over them.

Frank made his way to the chair, sat, adjusted his body until he was fairly comfortable, then dragged the knitted lavender afghan from the back of the chair and spread it out over him. A tad short for his long frame, it covered him from shoulders to knees.

For quite a while he sat there, his gaze glued to the woman and infant in the bed. But finally exhaustion overcame him and his eyelids drooped. He yawned, then closed his eyes and gave in to sleep.

Andrew was crying.

It's all right, baby. Mother's here. You're safe.

Leenie woke with a start. When she found Andrew wriggling against her, his little nose and mouth rooting at her breast, she sighed contentedly. *Thank you, God. Thank you for keeping my baby safe and bringing him home to me.*

"Hush, my darling," Leenie whispered. "Mommy will get you a bottle. It won't take a minute."

She got out of bed, then reached down and lifted a whimpering Andrew up and into her arms. Just as she turned around, she noticed Frank in the chair in the corner. She gasped. When had he come into her bedroom? He roused groggily from sleep and stood.

"Is he all right?" Frank asked, his voice husky.

Leenie had left the door to her room open, hoping Frank would come to her—come to her and Andrew and be a part of Andrew's homecoming. Apparently she'd fallen asleep before he'd joined them.

"He's fine. Just hungry." How was it that a man who needed a haircut and a shave and whose clothes always looked as if he slept in them could be so damned attractive? she wondered. And in the middle of the night, no less. "I have several bottles in the refrigerator. I'm taking Andrew with me to get one and warm it in the microwave."

"You stay here," Frank told her. "Let me get Andrew's bottle."

"All right. Thank you." Leenie began walking the floor with her whiny little boy. "But hurry, will you? Your son won't be patient for long. He wants what he wants when he wants it."

"Not unlike his father." Frank grinned. "By the way, how long do I heat the bottle in the microwave?"

"About forty-five seconds, then test it on the inside of your wrist. It should be warm, but not hot."

When Frank disappeared out into the hall, Leenie paced the floor, crooning to Andrew. How wonderful to hold him again. She kissed his little head. Ah, she loved his sweet smell.

By the time Frank returned—in three minutes flat—Andrew's whimpers had grown louder.

Her son had a big appetite and little patience.

"Here you go." Frank held out the bottle to her.

"Would you like to feed him?"

"Me?"

"You've already fed him once, right? You're an old pro now."

"Yeah, sure. I—"

"Sit back down in the chair and I'll hand him to you."

Frank did as she'd instructed. Then she placed Andrew in his arms. At first Andrew cried, apparently not happy about leaving his mother's arms. But when Frank stuck the nipple in his mouth, Andrew latched on and began sucking. Frank looked up at Leenie and smiled triumphantly.

"You're a natural," she told him.

"Am I?"

Her heart did a crazy rat-a-tat-tat. She wanted to wrap her arms around Frank and hug the life out of him. Didn't he have any idea how wonderful he was? Couldn't the big lug figure out that he was meant to be a family man? He was gentle, kind, loving and had so much to give to a woman and child. If only he wasn't so scarred from bad experiences with a selfish mother and an unfaithful wife. If only the two most important women in his life hadn't crippled him emotionally.

"The way you are with Andrew, a person would think you had vast experience with babies," Leenie said.

"I have zero experience with babies. It's Andrew. The way I feel about him makes it so easy to just—" Frank lifted his gaze from his son to Leenie. "I want to be a part of his life from now on."

She nodded. Emotion welled up inside her. Why hadn't she called Frank and told him the minute she found out she was pregnant?

"I called my boss at Dundee and asked for some time off. A week. I thought…that is if it's okay with you, I'd like to stay and get to know my son."

"Of course it's okay with me. I want you to be a part of Andrew's life."

"You won't have to put up with me permanently. Just for the next week or so." Frank looked down at Andrew. "I know a baby needs his mother, but when I'm between assignments, I'd like to come for visits. And maybe when Andrew is older, you might let him visit me in Atlanta."

Leenie clenched her teeth, then forced a smile, even though her heart was breaking. What had she expected? Not some confession of undying love. Not from Frank Latimer. He might love his son, but by God, he wasn't going to ever trust his heart to another woman, not even his son's mother. Not even to a woman who loved him so damn much that she could hardly stand it.

Smiling like an idiot, Leenie nodded and willed herself not to cry. She swallowed hard, then said, "Absolutely. You'll be welcome here any time. I want you to be a father to Andrew."

"Thanks, Slim." With Andrew nestled against him, Frank held the bottle securely in place while he leaned down and kissed his son's forehead.

Kate answered her cell phone on the first ring. She'd been waiting all night for this call.

"Hello."

"Kate?"

"Yes."

"I'm sorry it's taken me so long to get back to you, but I've had a lot going on here in Memphis. I guess Frank told you something about—"

"Frank doesn't really care about the FBI's great success," Kate said. "Andrew is all that matters to him."

"Yes, of course. That's understandable." Dante Moran hesitated for several moments. "I'm afraid I'm puzzled as to why you left me a message to call you. Is there some information Dundee needs in order to close out the case?"

"This wasn't an official Dundee case. This was a personal matter for Frank. Sawyer McNamara sent me along because…well, to be honest with you, Sawyer thought I might have a special interest in Andrew Patton's kidnapping."

"You've lost me. I don't understand why—"

"Eleven years ago my daughter was kidnapped and to this day I don't know what happened to her. I've searched for her for over a decade without any success. What I want to know is this—did y'all confiscate any files on the abducted children? Things like where they were born. State? Town? And dates. Dates of births? Dates they were adopted? Who adopted them?"

"You're asking me to divulge official FBI business," Moran said.

"All you have to say is yes or no."

"Yes."

Kate sucked in her breath. "How far back do those files go?"

"Rephrase that so I can give you a yes or no reply."

"Do they go back eleven years?"

"Yes."

Kate's heart lurched to her throat and for a moment she couldn't breathe. "Is there any way I can get a look at those files?"

"No."

"What if Sawyer McNamara—"

"No."

"You don't understand." Kate didn't mind begging. She'd gladly get down on her hands and knees and plead with him if she thought it would get her what she wanted. "Please. If there's even the slightest chance that my daughter was taken by the same abduction ring that stole Andrew—"

"I can't promise you anything. But I'll pull the files from ten years ago and take a look. I can't give you permission to see the files, but if you'll give me all the information on your daughter—''

''Mary Kate Winston. She was two months old. Blonde. Brown-eyed. Kidnapped from Prospect, Alabama. I can fax you all the details.''

''You do that.''

''How long—?''

''It could take days to find something…if there's anything to find.''

''I'm coming to Memphis,'' Kate told him. ''I'll give you the details of Mary Kate's abduction when I get there.''

''I'll be expecting you.''

''Moran?''

''Huh?''

''Thanks.''

''Don't thank me. I haven't done anything.''

''Oh yes you have. You've given me just a tiny bit of hope. I'm not sure why you're doing this for me. I don't think it's because you're such a nice guy, is it?''

''Hell no. Anybody who knows me will tell you I'm a real hard-ass.''

''Then why?''

''Don't look a gift horse in the mouth.''

''I'll leave for Memphis as soon as I can get packed.''

Leenie and Frank stood in the doorway, Andrew in Leenie's arms, and waved goodbye to Kate as she walked toward Frank's rental car parked in the driveway.

''Be careful driving in this rain,'' Leenie cautioned.

"The roads are probably still slippery from last night's sleet."

"I'll be very careful," Kate called back as she opened the car door.

"Call us when you get to Memphis," Frank said.

"Becoming a father has certainly turned you into the paternal type, hasn't it," Kate said jokingly, then slammed the door and started the car.

As soon as Kate backed out of the drive, Frank closed the door and turned to Leenie. "She'll be all right. I'm sure the roads are mostly clear by now. It's nearly ten o'clock."

"I'm not as concerned about her arriving safely to Memphis as I am about what she'll find out while she's there. If there is no information about her daughter in those files the FBI confiscated, she'll be heartbroken. She's been searching for her little girl for eleven years."

Frank slipped his arm around Leenie's shoulder, then tickled Andrew under his chin. "Everybody at Dundee knew there was something tragic in her past and some even speculated it had to do with a child, but none of us knew exactly what had happened."

"I can't imagine how she's stayed sane all these years," Leenie said. "And not only stayed sane, but actually functioned, kept a job, lived a fairly normal life and all. If I'd lost Andrew that way—"

"You didn't. He's right here, safe in your arms." Frank hugged her and their son to him. She slipped her free arm around Frank, trapping Andrew between them.

When Frank leaned over and kissed her on the mouth and then kissed Andrew on the top of his head, Andrew fussed loudly.

"I think we're crowding him," Frank said, a wide grin on his face. "So, Mama, what's the next thing on the agenda for today? Andrew's had his morning bottle and a diaper change, so what's next?"

"A bath. Want to give Andrew his bath?"

"Me?"

"Yes, you."

"Sure. No problem. How hard can it be to give a two-month-old a bath?"

Leenie smiled. Frank had a great deal to learn about babies.

Ten

Leenie prepared Andrew's bath, placing everything Frank would need in easy reach. Then she handed her son over to his father. Frank grinned confidently and laid Andrew on the changing table in the corner of the bathroom. Although Andrew whined softly, Frank managed to remove his son's sleeper and diaper before Andrew bellowed loudly.

Frank lifted Andrew in his arms, the baby's fat little naked body wriggling. "What's the matter big boy? Did Daddy not do it right? Is Mommy better at this than I am?"

When Andrew yelled even louder, his face turning red and tears pooling in his eyes, Frank turned to Leenie, who stood in the bathroom doorway. "Maybe you'd better—"

"No way." Leenie shook her head. "You can't change your mind at the last minute just because this is turning out to be a bit more difficult than you'd anticipated.'' When Frank frowned at her, she smiled. ''Remember, you're going to be around for only a week, so you need to cram a lot of experiences with Andrew into the time you'll have with him.''

Leenie was proud of herself for being able to joke with Frank about him leaving soon. Her pride demanded that he not know how much she wanted him to stay. If he didn't love her, she would be better off without him, wouldn't she? And she certainly wasn't going to use Andrew to hang on to a man who didn't want her.

Frank nodded. ''You're right.'' He carried a less-than-happy Andrew over to the bathroom sink filled with lukewarm bathwater, then shifted his son around in his arms several times. Once again he looked at Leenie. ''Maybe you'd better show me how to do this.''

Not budging an inch, Leenie said, ''Use your arm to support him, then ease him down into the water. The liquid soap and washcloth are right there on the vanity. And so is the shampoo. I usually wash his hair first, but if you prefer to leave that until last, it's okay.''

''No, we'll do this the way you always do it.''

Going by Leenie's instructions, Frank eased his son into the sink. Andrew quieted, but continued sniffing tiny sobs while Frank talked to him. Nonsensical words. Baby talk. It was all Leenie could do not to burst out laughing. If only the other Dundee agents could see him now, trying to support a baby in his bathwater with one arm while struggling with his other hand to open a bottle of shampoo. Finally after several attempts Frank managed to squirt a generous amount of shampoo into his hand.

"You know a guy needs at least four hands to do this." Frank wiped half the shampoo off on the vanity counter, then rubbed the rest into Andrew's hair.

Leenie watched while Frank scrubbed Andrew from top to bottom. And he was doing a pretty good job, too. Andrew cooperated fully, enjoying his bath—until Frank started to rinse the shampoo from his hair. The minute several drops of soapy water trickled down on his face, Andrew started screaming and thrashing. Water splashed everywhere. All over the vanity. Across the mirror behind the sink. And onto Frank, drenching his shirt and dampening his jeans.

"Help!" Frank called out. "I need reinforcements."

Chuckling softly, Leenie rushed in to assist him. "Here, let me take over."

The minute Leenie eased her arm around Andrew, Frank pulled back and moved out of her way. "Mommy to the rescue," Frank said to his son. "It's a good thing we've got her, isn't it?"

With practiced ease, Leenie soothed Andrew, then rinsed his hair and body thoroughly before lifting him up and out of the sink. Holding him with one hand, she picked up the hooded towel and wrapped him in it, covering his head with the hood. She turned to show Frank how easily the job had been accomplished, but instead stopped dead still and sucked in her breath.

Oh, jeez! Frank had stripped out of his shirt, leaving him bare to the waist. It just wasn't fair that he looked so damned appealing. Some men looked better with their clothes on. Not Frank Latimer. He definitely looked better without clothes. As a matter of fact, he was downright irresistible.

When he caught her ogling his muscular chest, he grinned. An electrified awareness passed between them. Leenie forced her gaze from his chest to his face.

"He's probably gotten you wet to the skin, too," Frank said, pointedly staring at her shirt, his gaze quickly zeroing in on the exposed right side of the damp cloth sticking to her breast. Andrew lay pressed to the left side, effectively concealing the other breast.

She swallowed. Her nipples tightened. "Why don't you put on a dry shirt while I get Andrew dressed." That said, she hurried out of the bathroom and straight to Andrew's nursery.

Escape! her mind screamed. *Get the hell away from Frank before he figures out how much you want him.* It was ridiculous the way her body reacted to him, to nothing more than him staring at her breast. If she gave in to her desires, she'd jump Frank the minute Andrew went down for a nap.

So, would that be so bad? she asked herself. *Yes, the logical part of her brain responded, you'd be a fool to fall into the sack with him. The guy's leaving in a week, running off to God knows where on his next assignment.* If she was smart, she'd keep Frank out of her bed and find a way to rip him out of her heart. When he left Maysville, he'd return to his life back in Atlanta. And that meant he'd be dating other women.

Gritting her teeth, Leenie growled inwardly, with only a murmured whine audible. She hugged her baby before laying him in the middle of his crib.

By the time Frank joined them in their son's room a few minutes later, she had dressed Andrew for the day in navy blue corduroy overalls and a light blue cotton knit shirt. Just as she pulled on his light blue socks and white booties, Frank came up behind her and looked over her shoulder. She felt the heat from his body as he stood there so very close, his chest brushing against her back. When she glanced over her shoulder to speak to him, she gasped when she realized he'd lowered his head so that they were nose to nose, only inches separating them. She sucked in her breath. They stared at each other, both momentarily transfixed. And then he gave her a quick kiss, a kiss that was over before she had a chance to react. Frank slipped his arm around her waist, then looked down in the crib at Andrew. Using his free hand, he reached out and tickled Andrew's belly.

"I hope you'll give your dad another chance," Frank said. "If Mommy will let me, I want to try giving you a bath tomorrow."

Clearing her throat, Leenie responded. "Of course you can try again tomorrow. You can do anything you want for and with Andrew while you're here. You can bathe him and give him his bottle. You can rock him, sing to him, walk the floor with him. And change his diapers. Both the wet ones and the dirty ones."

Frank groaned. "I'm not sure about the dirty ones. I might leave those to you."

"Ah, don't be a chicken. You want to teach your son to be brave, don't you? How's it going to look to him if years from now he finds out you were afraid of a dirty diaper?"

"Being a man himself, I figure he'll understand."

"Andrew will not be a chauvinist. He's going to

be the type of man who shares all the responsibilities for childcare with his wife.'' The moment she made the statement, she wished back the words. She couldn't retract what she'd said, no matter how much she'd like to. Had Frank misconstrued her perfectly innocent comment? Would he think she was hinting for a marriage proposal?

When Frank didn't say anything, was in fact extremely quiet, Leenie took a deep breath and said, ''That's a generalization, of course. I'm assuming Andrew will be married before he becomes a father.''

Frank cleared his throat. ''Yeah. We—er—it'll be a case of do as I say, not do as I did.''

Leenie groaned. ''Look, let's just lay our cards on the table, okay?'' She reached up and wound the Noah's Ark musical mobile hanging above the crib. ''We've been dancing around each other, around the subject of marriage and sharing custody of Andrew and his future...our futures.''

''I didn't want to rush you into making decisions right away.'' Frank stepped back, putting some distance between their bodies. ''I thought I was doing the right thing by not pushing you, by giving you time to recover from everything you've gone through lately.''

With Andrew contentedly gurgling and cooing as he watched the colorful animals circling above him and listening to the soft lullaby the mobile's music box played, Leenie turned to Frank. ''Let's step out in the hall.''

Frank stared at her with a puzzled expression on his face.

''Babies pick up on the moods of the adults in their

life, especially their mother's mood. In case either of us gets upset or talks a little too loud or—''

''Are we going to have an argument?''

''No, of course not. It's just…well, we might not agree on everything. And I'd rather Andrew not be exposed to our differences of opinion. Not now. And not in the future.''

Frank nodded. ''I agree.''

When Leenie walked out of the nursery and down the hall, Frank followed her. After pausing a few feet shy of her bedroom door, she confronted Frank.

''I don't want you to get the wrong impression,'' she told him. ''Or read anything into the comment I made.''

''What wrong impression?''

''About marriage.''

''I didn't read anything into your comment,'' he said. ''I hope Andrew is married when he becomes a father. It'll make his life and his child's much easier.'' Frank's gaze met hers. ''Not to mention his child's mother.''

''Hmm-mmm.'' Leenie blew out a long, huffing sigh. ''Let me be honest with you.'' *Yeah, sure, you're going to be honest with him.* Her conscience laughed at her lie. Okay, so she'd be honest with him, up to a point.

''By all means.'' Frank leaned closer, placed his open palm on the wall behind Leenie's head and looked directly into her eyes. ''Be honest with me.''

Leenie's knees went weak. Her heartbeat accelerated. ''I'm very fond of you. And I like you.'' *Oh, get real, Leenie. You're fond of him? You like him? You're not being exactly honest are you? Okay, so*

I'm hog-wild crazy about him. I love the big lug so much it hurts.

"I'm very fond of you, too." He didn't take his eyes off her. "And I've been surprised by the fact that I like you so much. Really like you. More than any woman…" He cleared his throat. "Let's just say I admire you."

He admired her? Well, at least that was something. "Ideally, I'd like to be married to my son's father, but—"

"That would be ideal for Andrew, for any kid, to have his parents married to each other. But having parents who are not married is much better than having married parents who fight all the time. Believe me, I know. My parents hated each other and my sister and I paid the price for every one of their battles."

"You're right, of course. Parents who don't love each other shouldn't be married."

"Sometimes even love isn't enough to keep people together. I loved Rita, but—"

"It usually is when both of them are in love."

Frank removed his hand from the wall and stood up straight. "Yeah, I suppose that's true."

The rather sad look on Frank's face touched her heart. She wanted to hug him to her and tell him that she'd never betray him the way Rita had, that he could trust her with his love.

"We don't have to rehash any of your bad memories. Your parent's horrible marriage. Your breakup with Rita. And I won't bore you with how many years I looked for Mr. Right and kept finding one Mr. Wrong after another. Nor will I go to great lengths to make you understand how important a family is to me since I grew up without a real family. But you do need to know that Andrew is the most important thing in my life and although I'm willing for you to be a part of his life—''

''But since we aren't married, I'll never be a full-time dad. You'll be his primary caretaker and some-day if…when you marry, your husband will be a full-time dad to my son.''

She stared at Frank, her mind trying to understand his reasoning. ''You've given this quite a bit of thought, haven't you?''

Frank stuck his hands in his pockets as if he needed to do something with them. ''Since we're being hon-est with each other…'' He grimaced, as if what he had to say pained him. ''The truth of the matter is that I hate the idea of Andrew having a stepfather.''

Leenie nodded. ''I understand. Believe me, I'd hate him having a stepmother.''

Frank grabbed her by the shoulders, his big, long fingers holding her firmly. ''I hate the idea of you with another man.''

Her eyes rounded in surprise. Her stomach muscles tightened. ''Frank?''

His mouth came down on hers possessively, claim-ing her completely. She responded immediately, re-turning his passion. When she lifted her arms to en-circle his neck, his hands skimmed either side of her waist and moved downward, settling on her hips. He pressed her against him. She gasped when she felt his erection.

Stop this while you still can, the sensible part of her mind told her. But it felt so good to be in Frank's arms, to have his mouth devouring hers, to know that he wanted her as desperately as she wanted him.

However, just because he didn't want another man to have her didn't mean he loved her. Remember that, she told herself.

If she succumbed to Frank every time he came back to Maysville to visit Andrew, she'd wind up living in limbo, always waiting for Frank, accepting him on his terms, taking whatever he was willing to give her. She simply couldn't live that way. She wanted more. Hell, she deserved better.

Ending the kiss, she shoved against his chest. He didn't stop immediately, but when she gave him a second and much harder shove, he halted, pulled back and glared at her.

"I can't," she told him.

"Leenie…"

She held both hands up between them, warning him off. "It's not that I don't want you. God knows I do. I want you so much. But even though you're Andrew's father and have every right to come in and out of his life from now on, I can't put my life on hold waiting for your visits, no matter how frequent they might be. I want more than a part-time lover, more than an on-again-off-again affair."

The vein in Frank's neck throbbed. His gaze narrowed as he studied her face intently. "Do you think holding out on me will make me propose? Is that it? You want me to marry you and you think I want to have sex with you so much that I'll—"

How dare he! To think he'd judge her so harshly, that he'd believe her capable of doing such a despicable thing. Leenie saw red. "Why you egotistical bastard, you!" She flung back her hand, instinctively preparing to attack.

Catching her by the wrist, Frank aborted the slap

midair. "I won't be manipulated, honey. I've played the puppet fool for women more masterful at the art than you. My mother led my father around by the nose for years and she used me and my sister to torment the hell out of him. And Rita—"

"Rita, Rita, Rita!" Leenie jerked free of his hold. "God, Frank, grow up, will you? Do you think you're the only person who had a rotten childhood? Do you think you're the only man who's ever let a woman make a fool of him? I made a mistake thinking you were strong and brave and fearless. Under that Dundee agent guise of yours, you're a coward. You're scared of me. You don't have the guts to love me, let alone marry me."

Frank opened his mouth to respond, but before he could, she tapped her finger on his chest repeatedly and shouted, "I wouldn't marry you if you were the last man on earth. Do you hear me, Frank Latimer? You're lousy husband material." She whirled around and ran to her bedroom.

Frank stood in the hallway, so stunned that he couldn't move or speak for several minutes. By the time he recovered, Leenie had slammed her bedroom door in his face and Andrew was crying at the top of his lungs.

Frank cursed softly under his breath as he stared at the closed door. Women! Hadn't she said she wanted them to be honest with each other? Apparently she hadn't meant what she'd said. Leenie wasn't any different from other women. All that mattered to her was what she wanted, what she needed. Well, he didn't want to get married and he sure as hell didn't need her. He didn't need any woman.

Andrew's cries grew louder. Frank banged on Leenie's bedroom door. "Andrew's crying."

"I'm not deaf," she shouted through the closed door.

"Aren't you going check on him?"

"You're his father, aren't you? You go see why he's crying."

"All right, I will."

Frank stomped off down the hallway, went into the nursery, marched over to his son's crib and looked down at the red-faced infant. "What's the matter? Did you hear your mother screaming at me?" Frank leaned over the crib, then reached down and lifted Andrew up and into his arms. He laid his son on his shoulder and patted his back lovingly. "It's all right. Don't cry. I think I just made a big mistake and I don't know how I'm going to fix it."

After several minutes of being petted and soothed, Andrew stopped crying and lay peacefully against his father.

"You might as well know it now, son—you'll never understand women."

After sulking in her room for a good fifteen minutes, Leenie eased open the door and peeked outside, making sure Frank wasn't waiting around for her. Since Andrew had stopped crying, she assumed Frank had managed to soothe their son.

Their son.

Frank was right about one thing—about the way squabbling parents had an adverse effect on kids. If they were going to work out an arrangement to share Andrew—and whether she wanted to or not, she knew it was the right thing to do—they had to find a way to be friends. Just not friends *and* lovers. She could not deal with an on-again-off-again affair.

Could she?

No! Absolutely positively not!

Opening the door wide, she scanned the hallway and saw no sign of Frank. She walked quietly down the hall to the nursery. The door was open, the room empty. Frank must have taken Andrew downstairs, she thought. He'd probably realized Andrew was hungry and he'd taken him to the kitchen to prepare a bottle.

Do what you have to do, she told herself. *Go find Frank and settle things with him. Convince him that you don't expect him to marry you, that it's not what you want. Lie to him? Yes, lie to him, if that's what it takes to make peace. For Andrew's sake.*

Leenie went to the living room, through the dining room and into the kitchen, but saw no sign of Frank and Andrew. Where were they? Surely Frank hadn't gone outside with Andrew, not in this freezing weather.

"Frank?" she called.

No response.

She rushed from room to room, searching the entire house, calling out Frank's name repeatedly. Realizing they weren't anywhere inside, Leenie grabbed her coat off the rack and rushed into the backyard. Empty. A few birds searched the frozen ground for food. A lone squirrel scurried across the fence and onto a low hanging limb.

"Frank Latimer, where are you?" she cried.

Silence.

She raced to the front yard. No sign of them. Then she opened the garage and stopped dead still when she saw her SUV was missing. Frank had taken Andrew! He'd put her baby in his car seat inside the Envoy and driven off with him. Without saying one word to her. Where the hell had Frank gone? How dare he run off with Andrew!

Calm down, Leenie, she told herself. *Frank has not kidnapped Andrew. You're overreacting. Take some deep breaths. Andrew is safe. He's with his father.*

Leenie sat down on the front step, pulled her knees up to her chest and hugged her arm around her legs as she rocked back and forth. *How could you do this to me, Frank?* she asked silently. *What were you thinking, taking Andrew without asking me?*

Andrew is all right. Frank will bring him back. Andrew is all right. Frank will bring him back. As she sat there, the frigid winter wind chilling her to the bone, Leenie kept reassuring herself. But deep down inside fear ate away at her, gradually eroding her belief that Frank would never actually take Andrew away from her.

The minute he turned the SUV into the driveway, Frank saw Leenie sitting on the steps and wondered why she was there instead of inside. It couldn't be much more than thirty-nine or forty degrees, with a wind chill factor of well below freezing. So what was she doing outside? Was something wrong? When she saw him, she jumped up and came running toward the Envoy, waving her arms and screaming something. Good God, what had happened? Instead of pulling into the garage as he'd planned, he stopped the vehicle in the driveway and rolled down his window.

"Where is Andrew?" Leenie cried."

"Shh." Frank put his index finger to his lips to

indicate silence, then nodded to the back seat where a sleeping Andrew rested comfortably in his car seat. "Don't wake him."

"Don't you dare tell me what to do!" she screeched at Frank as she jerked on the backdoor handle. "Open this damn door. I want my son!"

"What the hell's the matter with you?" Frank hit the button to unlock the doors, then opened his door and got out just as Leenie flung open the back door. He grabbed her half a second before she dove inside the SUV.

When he hauled her out of the Envoy, she fought him like a wild woman for a couple of seconds. He yanked her to him, then reached around her and closed the door quietly before her tirade woke Andrew.

"Tell me what's wrong?" he asked when she glared at him.

"You took Andrew away and I had no idea where you'd gone or if…if you'd bring him back. How dare you—"

Frank grasped her shoulders and shook her gently. "Calm down. You're nearly hysterical."

"I am not hysterical. How dare you take Andrew without telling me. You should have—"

"I left a note on the refrigerator. Didn't you see it? God, Slim, you're overreacting a bit, aren't you?"

"Overreacting my ass, you unfeeling, uncaring bastard! My son was kidnapped and for days I had no idea if he was dead or alive. And you just take him with you, without telling me. What was I supposed to think?"

Ah, hell. When she put it that way, she made sense. Frank hadn't given it a thought, taking Andrew with him to pick up lunch. He'd hoped that the meal could be a peace offering, had believed she'd see him providing lunch as a caring thing to do. The last thing he'd intended was to frighten Leenie. No wonder she was so upset.

He loosened his tight grip on her shoulders and looked into her teary eyes. "I'm sorry. God, honey, I'm so sorry. I didn't think. You have a right to call me every name in the book. I went to pick up lunch for us and since Andrew was a little fussy, I just took him and a bottle with me. I knew if I knocked on your bedroom door, you'd just holler at me again, so—"

"I panicked when I realized you'd taken Andrew. I didn't see the note you'd left."

"What I did was thoughtless. It was stupid."

"I—I did overreact."

He pulled her into his arms, then kissed her temple. "I'm sorry about all the things I said to you earlier. I know you'd never do what I accused you of doing. You're nothing like my mother or my ex-wife. Let's face it, I'm an idiot."

"You're not an idiot. You want us to be lovers and when I said no, you went with your gut reaction and thought I was trying to pull a fast one on you. I wasn't. I'd never do that."

"Yeah, I know. And you're right. I have a major problem with trusting a woman. And you're right about my wanting us to be lovers. But I'll settle for our being friends."

"Oh, Frank, don't you see—we can't be just friends. The sexual chemistry between us is too strong. We're already using Andrew as an excuse to bicker, when what we should do is—"

''Get married?''

''What? No, I mean—''

''Are you saying that if I asked you to marry me, you'd say no?''

''Yes. No. Oh, damn it, Frank, don't do this. You don't want to get married. Not to me. Not to anyone.''

''I want to be a full-time father to Andrew. I want to be a full-time lover to you. Do you have another solution, other than marriage?''

Eleven

"Let's postpone this talk until later," Leenie had told Frank. "Right now, all I want is to take Andrew inside and put him in his bed. I need to see him safe and sound in his own room, with me watching over him."

Frank had opened the door, removed Andrew from his car seat and handed him to her. "I'm sorry I upset you. I swear it'll never happen again. I won't even take Andrew from one room to another without asking you, if that's what you want."

How could she stay angry with Frank when he was so apologetic? And sincerely so. If she had trusted him, the thought that he might have taken Andrew away from her would never have entered her mind. But that was one of the problems between them—she and Frank didn't trust each other. He didn't trust women in general, and understandably so, after the numbers his mother and Rita had done on him. And trust was an issue with her, too. She didn't trust Frank not to hurt her, and he would, even though it really wouldn't be his fault. He couldn't help it if he didn't love her.

They spent the rest of the day together as a family. She and Frank had shared the chicken salads and freshly baked croissants he'd gone to the deli and bought for their lunch. And they'd talked about the future, about the pros and cons of marriage versus finding a way to share joint custody of Andrew. But they hadn't reached a decision, hadn't agreed on a solution to their problem. They both wanted what was best for Andrew, but couldn't decide exactly what that was.

When Andrew woke from his nap, Frank had changed his diaper and given him a bottle while she telephoned Debra to check on her progress.

"I should be able to leave the hospital the day after tomorrow," Debra had said. "Are you sure my coming to your house won't be a problem since Frank's still there?"

"Frank and I can sort through our problems just as easily with you here as we can alone."

"What's wrong? I hear something in your voice."

"Frank thinks maybe we should get married."

"That's wonderful," Debra had said.

"He thinks we should get married for Andrew's sake."

"That's not so wonderful."

No, that wasn't so wonderful. She loved Frank and wanted to be his wife. She'd like nothing better than to have him around all the time, for him to be a full-time father to his son. But what sort of life would it

be for them? How long would it take before Frank
started feeling trapped? And how long would it be
before he realized she was madly in love with him?
Sooner or later, she'd want more than great sex and
his admiration. And eventually her neediness would
push him further and further away from her.

The sun set early in December, making the days
short. Darkness descended somewhere around five
o'clock. While Frank sat on the floor beside Andrew,
who lay on a quilt staring up at his infant jungle gym,
and watching as his father played with the toy, Leenie
went around closing all the blinds and turning on
lamps throughout the house.

"Are you hungry?" she asked, standing across the
room watching Frank entertaining his son. "Want me
to open some cans and put together a bite of supper?"

"Yeah, I'm getting hungry, but why don't we just
order pizza?"

"Okay. What do you like on yours?"

"The works. Everything but anchovies."

"All right."

When Frank smiled at her, she returned his smile.
Suddenly the telephone rang. Leenie jumped.

"Want me to get it?" he asked.

"No, I'll get it. I'm just jittery from days of hoping
and praying the phone would ring and we'd hear good
news." She went over to the portable phone resting
on the desk near the windows, picked up the receiver
and said, "Hello, Patton residence."

"Leenie?"

"Haley?"

"Hey, girl. When can I come over and see my
godson?"

"Anytime you'd like. I was wondering why you hadn't already dropped by."

"I thought you and Frank might need some time alone with Andrew," Haley said. "Besides, I'm having some problems here at the station and I'll be stuck here until I can find a replacement for your replacement on tonight's show."

"What happened to Dr. Bryant?"

"An emergency appendectomy around two this afternoon."

"What about Megan Vickers?"

"Called her office. She's out of town."

"You know, Haley, I could come in just for tonight."

"Could you? No. Forget it. You're not ready to come back to work."

Frank eased Andrew out from under the plastic jungle gym and lifted him into his arms.

"What's wrong?" he asked.

"Wait just a minute, will you, Haley?" She placed her hand over the mouthpiece and looked at Frank. "Dr. Bryant had an emergency appendectomy this afternoon and Haley can't find someone to do my talk show tonight. Do you think you can handle Andrew alone for about three hours so I could—"

"Do you trust me to look after him?"

Their gazes met and locked. Good question. Did she trust Frank? Did she trust him to take care of Andrew? Did she trust him to not run off with their son?

"Yes, I trust you," she told him.

For a fraction of a second she noticed something in Frank's eyes, in his expression, something that made her heart flutter and her stomach do flip-flops.

The smile playing at the corners of his mouth widened into an ear-to-ear grin.

"If you'd rather, Andrew and I can come to the station with you."

"Oh, that would be— No, that's unnecessary. It's freezing cold outside and Andrew will be asleep by eight and…no, you keep him here."

"All right. Tell Haley you'll do the show tonight."

She removed her hand from the mouthpiece. "Haley, I'll be at the station by eleven-thirty."

Andrew went to sleep early. At seven-twenty. Odd, she thought, since her son was a little creature of habit and took his naps at regular times, ate on schedule and went to sleep for the night between eight and eight-fifteen every evening. He'd been doing this for weeks before the kidnapping. There's nothing to worry about, she told herself. Being stolen from Debra's car and taken care of by strangers for days on end was the probable cause in his change of habit.

Frank, who'd been holding Andrew when he fell asleep, laid their baby down in his crib, then turned to Leenie. "If there's anything you need to do to get ready for tonight's broadcast, go ahead. I'll listen for Andrew in case he wakes up."

"Thanks. I'd like a long, hot soak in the bathtub. I need to come up with a topic to present tonight. Although it's been only a week since I did my last show, it feels as if it's been months."

"Go take your bath," he told her. "I'm going to watch a little TV. But I'll keep the baby monitor with me so I can hear Andrew if he so much as whimpers."

"You know what I wish you'd do before you settle down in front of the TV?"

"What? Just name it."

"Call Kate."

"She said she'd call us if...when she found out something."

"I know, but I just want to hear from her. And I want her to know that we're thinking positive thoughts for her."

"Okay, I'll see if I can get in touch with her."

Leenie slipped into her gold silk robe and matching house slippers after drying off and wrapped a towel around her wet hair. She'd decided that her topic for tonight's radio show would be "Dealing with Issues of Trust." She'd present a list of facts stated by other professionals from their various published works and then she'd give the listeners a chance to call in. It was during those discussions with her audience that the programs came alive. And in all honesty, it was when she came alive, too. God, she loved her job.

After towel drying her hair, she tossed the towel into the hamper and exited the bathroom. The house was quiet, almost too quiet. When she opened her bedroom door, she heard humming, then singing. A deep baritone voice crooning softly. Had Andrew awakened and Frank was trying to get him back to sleep? Leenie walked down the hall until she reached the open nursery door.

Shirtless and shoeless, Frank stood in the middle of the room, a half-awake Andrew pressed against his naked chest. Leenie stood there, spellbound, her gaze glued to Frank's face. He was looking at his son with such overwhelming love. And fascination. It was so obvious that he was in awe of the child they had created together.

Leenie's heart caught in her throat.

Frank kept humming and kept staring adoringly at Andrew, completely unaware that Leenie was watching him. After a good four or five minutes, Andrew's eyes closed completely and Frank laid him down in his crib. He leaned over and kissed Andrew. And tears lodged in Leenie's throat.

Frank turned around, then halted abruptly when he saw Leenie standing in the doorway. "He woke up and fretted a little bit, so I gave him a bottle and tried rocking him. But he kept fighting going back to sleep. When I started walking around with him and singing to him, he quieted down."

"You're spoiling him."

"Is that a bad thing?"

"No, it most certainly isn't. I think a little spoiling is essential for every child, don't you?"

"Absolutely."

Frank kept his gaze linked with hers as he walked toward her. "We created something pretty great when we made that little boy."

"Yes, we did. He's the best of both of us, isn't he?"

Frank reached out and caressed her cheek. "Leenie, I—"

It was happening again, just like it did every time he touched her. All that wild and crazy magic between them couldn't be controlled. But she had to control it or she'd wind up giving in to him, and not just for tonight. If she wasn't careful, she'd wind up agreeing to marry him and then where would they be? She'd be deliriously happy for a while and maybe

Frank would be, too. But he'd be marrying her for the wrong reason and eventually he'd want out. Wasn't it better to end things now than later, after she and Andrew had grown accustomed to having Frank in their lives all the time?

"Did you call Kate?" Leenie asked, determined to ease the sexual tension sizzling between them.

"Uh, yeah, I called. She said to tell you hi and to give Andrew a hug from her."

"Has she found out anything?"

"Nope. She told me that Moran has promised he'll share any information he finds that might be linked to Mary Kate, but it could take weeks to find anything. And there's always the chance that Kate's daughter wasn't taken by the infant abduction ring."

"Poor Kate. When I think about what she's gone through—"

Frank cupped Leenie's face with his hands. "Don't think about it. Just be grateful that we got Andrew back so quickly, that he's safe here with us. With his mother and father."

Don't look at me that way, she wanted to shout at him. His gaze devoured her hungrily, as if he was starving and she was a bountiful feast laid out before him. Every feminine instinct within her cried out for him to take her, to make her his. But logic dictated the exact opposite. If she wanted to save herself, she needed to get away from him. Now!

"Go back to watching TV," she told him as she turned away and headed down the hall. "I have things to do—"

He caught up with her, grabbed her arm and whirled her around to face him. "I know all the reasons why we shouldn't, but I don't give a damn. I want you, Slim. And I know you want me.''

"Oh, Frank. Of course I want you, but—''

He placed his index finger over her lips to silence her.

She looked pleadingly into his eyes.

His broad shoulders lifted and fell. He nodded, then released her and turned away, without saying a word. She stood there and watched him leave her. And that's what it felt like—it felt like he was leaving her, not just at this moment, but forever.

"Frank!''

He halted, but didn't turn around, simply standing at the end of the hallway.

She blurted out, "I know I'll regret it later, but…''

He turned to face her, a hopeful expression on his face.

She ran toward him. He caught her in his arms and lifted her off her feet. She flung her arms around his neck and held on as he lowered his head to kiss her. Maybe she was a fool—a fool in love—but she didn't care. *Don't think about tomorrow,* she told herself. *Don't worry about the future. You have this precious moment. Don't waste it.*

Frank carried her into her bedroom, slid her down his body and onto her feet. With nervous need, she touched his chest. Kissed him. Tasted him. Smelled him. When she reached his jeans, she popped the snap and lowered the zipper, then slid her hand inside to fondle his sex. He was hard. Ready for her. He helped her get rid of his jeans and briefs, then stood very still when she ran her hands over him from hips to knees and slowly made her way back up. Leenie dropped to her knees in front of him. He held his breath when she touched him intimately. When her tongue replaced her fingertips, he groaned with pleasure. She laved him from root to tip, then took him into her mouth. Frank speared his big fingers through her hair and held her head in place while she titillated him.

And when he was on the verge, he yanked her to her feet, ripped open her robe and gazed at her breasts, at her flat belly and at the thatch of golden hair between her thighs. Her body tingled, her nerves zinging with anticipation. Her femininity clenched and unclenched as moisture gathered in preparation. He slid the robe off her shoulders. The gold silk pooled at her feet.

Frank kissed her neck, her throat and each shoulder, before lowering his head to first one breast and then the other. Already aroused unbearably, Leenie keened when he suckled her breast, his tongue tormenting her nipple. Her back arched. She grasped his muscular biceps and her nails bit into his flesh. His mouth on her breasts, moving back and forth from one to the other, drove her mad. He cupped her hips and pulled her up and against his erection. Pure electricity shot through her when he drove his tongue into her mouth at the same time he lifted her by her hips so that he could thrust up inside her. Yowling with earthshattering intensity, she wrapped her legs around his waist.

With their bodies joined intimately, Frank walked backward toward the bed, then toppled them over and onto the plush cotton sheets. He hammered into her repeatedly. Leenie responded with upward lunges, wild with her own need. They went at one another with animalistic passion. Kissing. Licking. Nipping.

The tension wound tighter and tighter inside Leenie until she thought she'd splinter into a million pieces, but each time she reached the brink, Frank would pull back just enough to stop the inevitable. And after she had a chance to catch her breath, he'd begin the sensual attack again until she was out of her mind, wanting, needing, begging him for release.

He lifted her buttocks, bringing her as close as possible and then plunged to the hilt, burying himself deeply inside her. She clung to him, maneuvering herself so that each jab gave her pleasure and suddenly with one final thrust, she came apart. Fulfillment burst inside her. The sensations went on and on, until only the sweet aftershocks remained. And as those remaining tingles floated through her body, Frank increased his speed, pounding harder and faster. He growled, then shuddered as he jetted into her.

Afterward he slid to her side and they lay there together, breathing hard, staring up at the ceiling. He inched his hand over to hers and clasped it firmly. She sighed with contentment. And in that moment she realized that lovemaking would never be this way with anyone else. Only with Frank. Because she loved Frank, as she would never love another man.

Twelve

After Leenie left for the studio, Frank wandered around the house, returning again and again to Andrew's nursery. He wanted to take care of his son, wanted to provide for him. And he wanted to make sure that even if something happened to him Leenie and Andrew would be provided for. He wasn't a multimillionaire by any means, but when his father died, he'd inherited close to half a million dollars, which he'd divided between investments and one-hundred-percent-safe certificates of deposit. The first thing he wanted his lawyer to do was set up a college fund for Andrew. After that he needed to adjust his will. All of this could wait till morning, of course. He intended to call his lawyer first thing tomorrow and let him get busy on the paperwork. He'd have to fly back to Atlanta sooner than he'd planned to sign the papers, to lease his apartment and to hand in his resignation.

Sawyer might release him immediately, if he wasn't needed on another assignment. If that were the case, he'd use the final assignment as the equivalent of his two weeks' notice.

He might be jumping the gun a bit by making all these plans. Leenie hadn't agreed to marry him. Not yet. But she hadn't been able to come up with an arrangement that made more sense. If anyone had told him that he'd ever even remotely consider remarrying, he'd have told them they were crazy. He'd sworn to himself that after the fiasco with Rita, he'd stay single to his dying day. But that was before Andrew.

Admit it, Latimer, Andrew is only a part of this equation. You actually want to marry Leenie. You like the idea of being with her every day for the rest of your life.

So what would it take to persuade Leenie to accept his proposal? Would he have to get down on bended knee?

Come to think of it, he never did actually propose. He'd asked her if she knew another solution to their problem other than marriage. That sure hadn't been romantic. No wonder she hadn't been overly thrilled by his suggestion. Women liked romance. Leenie probably expected a diamond and a fancy dinner and— He'd have to take care of those things, too, when he went to Atlanta. But he wanted everything to be a surprise. So, how was he going to work it? He'd have to figure out something so she wouldn't suspect what he had planned.

And what will you do if after all your best laid plans, she tells you thanks but no thanks? He'd camp on her doorstep and wear her down, that's what he'd do. He had no intention of taking no for an answer.

Leenie woke at ten-thirty the next morning when the telephone rang insistently. Where's Frank? she wondered. She'd arrived home from the station at two-forty this morning and found Frank asleep in the rocker in Andrew's room. She hadn't had the heart to wake him, but sometime before dawn, he'd crawled in bed with her and snuggled close. They'd made slow, sweet love and then had fallen asleep.

Damn, why didn't he answer the phone? She came awake groggily, reached over and picked up the receiver from the bedside phone.

"Hello?"

"May I speak with Frank Latimer?" a male voice asked.

"Who may I say is calling?"

"Steve O'Neal. I'm his lawyer."

Leenie's eyes popped wide open. "And this is in reference to?"

"Is this Ms. Patton?" the man asked.

"Yes, it is."

"Then I'm sure Frank's told you about his plans for Andrew."

Frank had plans for Andrew? What plans? "Yes, of course he's told me."

"I have to admit that I was totally surprised by Frank's news that he's a father. Never saw old Frank in that role. But he doesn't seem to have any doubts about being a full-time father to his son."

Leenie's heart sank. Frank intended to be a full-time father? When had he gotten in touch with his lawyer? Had he called this Mr. O'Neal and told him that he wanted full custody of Andrew? No! Frank wouldn't do that. But what other reason would Frank need a lawyer to handle anything concerning Andrew?

"Hold on, please, Mr. O'Neal, and I'll get Frank."

Leenie laid the phone on the nightstand, got out of bed, slipped into her robe and searched from room to room. She found Frank in the kitchen scrambling eggs and frying bacon. Safe in his infant carrier placed in the middle of the kitchen table, Andrew contentedly watched his father.

"What are you doing?" she asked.

"Morning, Slim. I'm fixing your breakfast. I had planned to bring it to you on a tray, but now that you're up, I'll serve it to you at the table."

"Didn't you hear the phone ringing?"

"Yeah, but I sort of had my hands full, so I figured I'd let the answering machine get it." His broad, infectious smile prompted an involuntary smile from her. "Damn, I didn't unplug the phone in the bedroom, did I? I'd meant to do that, so if it rang it wouldn't wake you, but—"

"The call is for you," she told him. "It's a Mr. O"Neal."

"Oh, yeah. He's a, uh, er, a friend from Atlanta."

Leenie kept her smile in place by sheer force of will. If Frank had nothing to hide, why hadn't he admitted that Mr. O'Neal was his lawyer? Whatever business about Andrew he needed to discuss with his attorney apparently was something he didn't want her to know about. So what could she construe from that?

"Look, honey, everything's ready—even the coffee. All you have to do is put the bacon, eggs and toast on a plate. I won't be on the phone long. You enjoy breakfast and I'll clean up when I get back."

He gave her a hurried kiss as he passed by her on

his way out of the kitchen. The minute he went out the door, she slumped into a kitchen chair and turned to her son.

"I think your father might be up to something." Leenie sighed. "The problem is I'm not sure what. If I trusted him, I wouldn't be filled with all these doubts, would I? When he comes back, I'll ask him. I'll come right out and tell him I want to know what's going on."

Andrew gurgled and cooed. Leenie groaned. Would she have to marry Frank to stop him for trying to get custody of Andrew? Maybe he'd contacted a lawyer because he wanted partial custody. But that wasn't what he'd told her. He'd agreed that while he was an infant, Andrew needed to be with her. So, what had changed Frank's mind? Did he intend to give her a choice—either marry him or he'd take Andrew away from her?

Don't be ridiculous, she told herself. Frank would never— She had to trust him. Had to believe in him. But could she marry him, knowing he didn't love her? It's what she wanted, wasn't it? Wasn't it possible that he'd fall in love with her after they married? It could happen, couldn't it?

Frank came back in the kitchen ten minutes later, after talking to Steve and then placing a call to Sawyer, who'd accepted his resignation over the phone and wished him the best of luck.

"I'm flying back to Atlanta this afternoon," Frank had told Sawyer. "I've got some legal papers to sign and an engagement ring to buy. And there's my apartment, I need to get rid of it, but I doubt I'll be able to get out of my lease."

"Geoff Monday's looking for a place," Sawyer had said. "He'd probably be glad to sublet the apartment from you until your lease is up."

Leenie sat at the table sipping coffee and pushing her scrambled eggs around on the plate. It didn't look as if she'd eaten a bite.

"What's wrong, Slim, aren't you hungry?" Frank asked. "Or don't you like my eggs?"

She offered him a fragile smile. "Just not hungry, I guess."

"Hey, look, I've got something to tell you."

Her smile widened. "Yes, what is it?"

"I have to fly back to Atlanta this afternoon."

"What?"

"I'll be gone only a couple of days," he said. "I'll be back before you know I'm gone."

"Why do you have to leave? I thought you planned—"

"Plans change. I—I've got some business for Dundee to take care of and—"

"Does Mr. O'Neal have something to do with your change of plans?"

"In a way." Frank came up behind her chair, leaned over, lifted her hair and kissed the nape of her neck. "Miss me a little while I'm gone."

"Frank, maybe we should talk some more about getting married. We never did resolve the issue, did we? I've been thinking about all the reasons I'm reluctant to rush into marriage and—"

"We can talk about our future plans when I get back from Atlanta." He gave her shoulders a caressing squeeze. "If I'm going to catch my plane, I need to hustle."

"I wish you didn't have to go."

"I'll be gone two days, tops."

She looked up at him with those shimmery blue eyes of hers and he thought he'd lose it. She had to be the prettiest thing on God's green earth. And if he played his cards right and didn't screw up again, she just might be his for the rest of their lives. But he had to do this thing right. He had to prove to her that they could make a lifelong commitment work. Okay, so she wanted romance and lovey-dovey stuff and he wasn't good at playing Prince Charming. But he could damn well try, couldn't he? And even if all they had going for them was great sex and Andrew, that would be enough, wouldn't it? Who knew, maybe love would come later for both of them.

"How about you and Andrew go with me to the airport?" he asked, wanting to be with them as long as possible. What he really wanted was to ask her to bring Andrew and come to Atlanta with him. But he'd be so damn busy that she might feel neglected.

"Why don't you just call a cab," she suggested. "We can say our goodbyes here and I won't have to get Andrew out in the cold."

"Sure." There was something bothering Leenie, but he couldn't imagine what. Maybe he should ask her about it. No, he'd just let it wait until he came back. If he didn't get a move on, he'd miss his flight and the sooner he went to Atlanta and set his house in order, the sooner he could come back to Leenie and Andrew.

Leenie had been stewing for two and a half days. Frank had called a couple of times each day and he'd been all sweetness and light, telling her how much he missed Andrew and her. And for the entire time he'd been gone, she had fought her inner demons—distrust and fear.

She had come to realize that it wasn't so much that she didn't trust Frank as that she wouldn't allow herself to believe that everything would work out all right for them. She'd had such rotten luck in her life. First her mother had died and a few years later her father. She'd been bounced around from foster home to foster home until she'd been sent to live with the Schmales. And in the happily ever after department, her love life had been a dismal failure. She'd had her heart battered and bruised several times before Frank Latimer finally broke it in so many pieces that it could never be mended.

Leenie was afraid to believe anyone could love her. And that's what it all boiled down to in the end. Frank was afraid to love because love had hurt him so badly in the past. And despite what her brilliant, logical mind told her, Leenie had somehow convinced herself that no man would ever truly love her. Certainly not Frank.

"Come on tater-tot," Leenie said as she lifted Andrew into her arms. "Your daddy is coming home today and we're going to the airport to meet him."

Ever since Frank had telephoned her to let her know he'd be arriving in Maysville around two-thirty, she had been debating what to do.

"I wish you'd come to the airport to meet me. You and Andrew. I'm flying in on the Dundee jet," he'd told her.

Not knowing what to expect when she arrived at the airport, Leenie buckled Andrew into his car seat in the back of her Envoy. Debra stood in the doorway, waving and smiling, as if she were seeing them off on some fabulous adventure. As a matter of fact, Debra had been entirely too cheerful since she'd come home from the hospital and whenever Leenie had complained about Frank's behavior, Debra had defended him. Was it because Debra wanted Leenie to marry Frank? Debra was just old-fashioned enough to think that a child's parents should be married. Or did Debra know something she didn't know?

Fifteen minutes after leaving her house, Leenie pulled into a parking slot at Maysville's small airport. What would she do if Frank asked her to marry him? What if he gave her only two choices—marry him or he'd take her to court over Andrew's custody?

"Let's go find out what Daddy's got up his sleeve." Leenie removed Andrew from his car seat, pulled the hood of his quilted coat over his head and took him out of the SUV.

After wrapping Andrew in a thick blanket to block out the crisp December wind, she hurried into the airport terminal and checked at the arrival desk to see if the private Dundee jet was expected to be on time.

"Yes, ma'am, that aircraft will be landing in approximately four minutes. By the way, are you Dr. Patton?"

"Yes, I'm Lurleen Patton."

"The pilot radioed ahead to ask that Dr. Patton—" the clerk smiled at Andrew "—and her son be escorted to the airplane."

"Oh, I see." Frank had been awfully sure she'd show up, hadn't he? "Well, all right. Exactly what do we do?"

"Just follow me. You'll be driven out on the runway and personally taken to the plane."

"I don't understand, but—"

"Come along. By the time we get outside, the plane will have landed."

Keeping Andrew cuddled against her, Leenie went along for the ride. Literally. In less than five minutes, when she stepped out of the cart that had delivered them to the Dundee jet, Frank Latimer appeared at the top of the steps. He waved at her, then rushed down the steps toward her.

She gasped when he wrapped his arm around her and urged her toward the steps. "Come on, Slim, I want to show you and Andrew the Dundee jet."

"Frank, what's going on? Nothing has made any sense to me since the day you left."

"Just come on board and I'll explain everything." When she eyed him skeptically, he said, "I promise."

She allowed him to escort her up the steps and into the airplane. Once inside, she skidded to a halt. The sleek, luxuriously decorated interior had been filled with flowers. Soft music wafted through the lounge. A bottle of champagne chilled in a silver bucket, flanked by two crystal flutes.

"What—what is all this?" she asked.

"It's a romantic setting," Frank told her.

"Yes, I guess it is, but—"

Frank reached out and took Andrew from her, removed their son's coat and placed him in an infant carrier lying in one of the ultraplush seats. "You sit there and be quiet for a few minutes, okay, pal? Daddy's got something very important to do."

Frank came back to Leenie, knelt down on one knee in front of her and clasped her hand. She felt as if her head was spinning.

"Leenie, will you marry me?"

"What?"

"I want you to marry me. I want us to build a life together."

He was proposing to her. Wasn't this what she'd wanted? And he'd set the scene for his proposal. He'd thought of just about everything.

"You want us to get married for Andrew's sake," she said.

Frank dug in his rumpled jacket pocket, pulled out a midnight blue velvet box and flipped open the lid. A sparkling diamond solitaire glistened against the dark blue bed.

"I went to half a dozen jewelers in Atlanta before I found the right one." He removed the ring from the box, lifted Leenie's left hand and slid the ring on her finger. She looked at the two-carat diamond and then stared down into Frank's smiling face.

"What will you do if I say no?" she asked, and held her breath waiting for his reply.

He laughed. "I'd die of a broken heart," he said jokingly.

"No, Frank, I'm serious." She tugged on his shoulders, urging him to stand.

His smile vanished. "I thought you—"

"If I refuse to marry you, what will you do?"

"Leenie, I'm confused by your question."

"I know that Steve O'Neal is your lawyer and that whatever legal matters he was taking care of for you had to do with Andrew. Do you plan to take me to court to get your rights as Andrew's father? Is that what you'll do if I won't marry you?"

Frank stared at her as if she'd suddenly grown an extra head. "I had Steve set up a college fund for Andrew. And I revised my will, leaving the estate I inherited from my father to Andrew and you." He grasped Leenie's shoulders. "Have you been fretting ever since I left Maysville thinking I was going to… My God, Slim, how could you think I'd ever try to take Andrew away from you?"

"I'm sorry. I—I just didn't know what to think."

"Don't you know I'd never do anything to hurt you? Hell, look at me, will you? I quit my job at Dundee, I sublet my apartment, I arranged my financial affairs so you and Andrew would be taken care of if anything ever happened to me. And I borrowed the Dundee jet to whisk us off to Las Vegas to get married. I bought out half a florist shop and spent a small fortune on that ring." His gaze jumped from the ring to Leenie's face. "What does that tell you?"

"It tells me that you really want to marry me."

"Is that all it tells you?"

"That you wanted everything to be romantic and special for me?"

"And?" He shook her gently. "Damn it, woman, don't you know when you've won?"

She jerked away from him. "Exactly what have I won? Marriage to you? Does that mean you've lost? If you think for one minute that I'm going to marry you just because—"

He grabbed her and kissed her, effectively ending her tirade.

When they finally came up for air, Frank said, "You're going to make me say it, aren't you?"

Leenie gasped silently as realization dawned. Frank Latimer was hers. She could see it in his eyes. He hadn't proposed simply because he wanted to provide a family for their son.

"Say what?" she asked, grinning, barely able to keep from laughing.

"Hell, Slim, you won my heart. Not that it's such a grand prize, but it's yours. All yours."

She slipped her arms around his neck, then lifted her left hand to look at her engagement ring. "If I've won your heart, does that mean you love me?"

Frank cleared his throat. "Yeah, I guess it does."

"Tell me."

"I just did."

"No you didn't. I want to hear the words."

"What about you?" he asked.

"What about me?"

"Do you love me?"

Leenie laughed. Joyously. Closing her eyes for just a second, she said a silent thanks to God. "Of course I love you, you big lug. I've been head over heels in love with you since the first time we made love."

Andrew gurgled loudly several times. Frank and Leenie looked at their son.

Frank shook his head. "Okay, son, okay. I know what I've got to do." Frank pulled Leenie close, gazed down into her eyes and said, "I love you, Leenie. But I have no idea how long I've loved you or when I realized that I did. I'm not sure. Maybe it was when I was in Atlanta whirling around, making plans. Or maybe it was just a few minutes ago when I saw you again."

"I think you've been in love with me since that first night." She brushed his lips breezily.

"Maybe I have."

"Maybe." She kissed him again. "We're going to have a wonderful life—you, me and Andrew."

"If we don't, it won't be for lack of trying." He kissed her. "We've got everything going for us."

"Including love."

"Especially love."

Epilogue

Leenie and Frank celebrated their first anniversary in style, surrounded by family and friends in their new house. They had designed the house themselves and worked with the contractor for eight long months until their dream became a reality. And during that time, Frank had designed several other projects, from a new garage for Haley and her husband to an addition for the pastor's home. While Leenie found job fulfillment in her TV and radio shows on WJMM, Frank was putting to use his heretofore unused college degree in architecture.

They had moved into their sprawling, bilevel, modern brick-and-glass structure shortly after Andrew's first birthday a little over two months ago. The day this house became their home, they'd had their own private party in front of the fireplace in their bedroom, a night neither of them would ever forget.

This year with Frank had been the happiest of her life. He let her know every day how much he loved her. An affair that had begun as a one-night stand had miraculously turned into a love affair that had healed two wounded souls and mended two battered hearts.

When Debra produced a piece of the wedding cake she had saved from the reception Leenie's friends had given them upon their return from their Las Vegas wedding, Frank accepted the plate and fork. He sliced off a piece of cake and put it in Leenie's mouth, then took a bite himself. Their guests clapped and cheered and Haley called for a speech.

Frank looked to Leenie. She shrugged. He leaned down and murmured in her ear, "Do you want me to tell all these people that I'm the happiest man on earth?"

Leenie slid her arm around his waist and hugged her husband. "You could, if you want to," she whispered. "But I think they already know that. Just as they know I'm mad about you and I'm deliriously happy."

"I could tell them that Andrew is the best-looking, smartest, most athletic one-year-old in the world, but that wouldn't be news either, would it?"

"Nope. Andrew's perfection is a well-known fact here in Maysville."

"Then we really don't have a speech to give them, do we? There's nothing we can tell them that they don't already know."

Leenie kissed Frank in front of their guests, which

actually made him blush and brought another round of cheers from their friends. ''I have a secret that I can tell you and then you can share it with everyone else.''

''You've got a secret?'' Frank said, not bothering to keep his voice low.

''Mmm-hmmm.''

''What's your secret?'' Haley Wilson shouted.

Once again Leenie whispered in her husband's ear.

''We're what?'' Frank said rather loudly. ''Are you sure?''

Smiling exuberantly, Leenie nodded.

''Hey, everybody, we're going to have another baby,'' Frank announced. ''In about six and a half months.'' When he calmed down a bit, he hugged Leenie to him and said softly, ''It happened the first night we spent in this house, didn't it?''

''Probably.''

Frank hugged her again. ''Are you all right? Is everything okay? With you and the baby? Is there anything I need to do for you?''

''I'm fine. The baby's fine. But I won't mind getting lots of TLC from my husband. After all, being pregnant at forty—''

''Slim, I'm going to give you enough TLC with this pregnancy to make up for what you missed when you were carrying Andrew. This time around, you can count on me every minute of every day. I'm not going to miss anything. I promise that I'll—''

Leenie covered his mouth with her open palm to quiet him, then reached down and took his hand in hers. "Just promise me that you'll love me forever. That's all I want. All I'll ever want."

"I'll love you forever," he vowed.

And Leenie knew he meant what he'd said. She trusted Frank as he did her. Trusted him with her heart, believing fully that at long last they had been blessed with the happily ever after love that neither of them had thought they'd ever find.

* * * * *

*Look for the next book in
Beverly Barton's exciting series,
THE PROTECTORS,
coming in August from Silhouette Desire!*

Who says lightning never strikes twice?

HELEN R. MYERS
WHILE OTHERS SLEEP

**Campbell Cody has twice experienced the strike of
lightning, and both times proved to be a deadly portent
of things to come. This time, Maida Livingstone, the dear
old woman she was hired to protect, has disappeared.**

**Jackson Blade has also lost someone: a teenage girl
he was tracking as part of a drug investigation.**

**Realizing their separate investigations are leading down
the same path, Campbell and Jackson join forces to expose
a killer. For Campbell, the encounter is as powerful as
a bolt of lightning. But will it prove as dangerous?**

"Colorful characters, tightly plotted storytelling
and a well-paced mystery..."
–*Romantic Times* on *No Sanctuary*

*Available the first week of April 2004
wherever paperbacks are sold.*

COMING NEXT MONTH

#1579 THE BOSS MAN'S FORTUNE—Kathryn Jensen
Dynasties: The Danforths
Errant heiress Katie Fortune had left home and her oppressive lifestyle
behind and began anew—as secretary to Ian Danforth. The renowned
playboy was a genius in the boardroom. But it was his bedroom
manner that Katie couldn't stop fantasizing about....

#1580 THE LAST GOOD MAN IN TEXAS—Peggy Moreland
The Tanners of Texas
She'd come to Tanner's Crossing looking for her family. What
Macy Keller found was Rory Tanner, unapologetic ladies' man. Rory
agreed to help with Macy's search—to keep an eye on her. But as the
sexual tension began to hum between them, it became difficult to keep
his *hands* off her!

#1581 SHUT UP AND KISS ME—Sara Orwig
Stallion Pass: Texas Knights
Sexy lawyer Savannah Clay was unlike any woman he'd ever known.
Mike Remington hadn't believed she'd take him up on his marriage
proposal—if only for the sake of the baby he'd inherited. Falling into
bed with the feisty blonde was inevitable; it was falling in love that
Mike was worried about....

#1582 REDWOLF'S WOMAN—Laura Wright
When Ava Thompson had left Paradise, Texas, four years ago, she'd
carried with her a little secret. But her daughter was not so little
anymore. Unsuspecting dad Jared Redwolf was blindsided by the
truth—and shaken by the power Ava had over him still. Could the
passion they shared see them through?

#1583 STORM OF SEDUCTION—Cindy Gerard
Tonya Griffin was a photographer of the highest repute...and
Web Tyler wanted her work to grace the pages of his new magazine.
But Web also had other plans for the earthy beauty...and they didn't
involve work, but the most sensual pleasures.

#1584 AT ANY PRICE—Margaret Allison
Kate Devonworth had a little problem. Her small-town paper needed
a big-time loan, and her childhood crush turned wealthy investor
Jack Reilly was just the man to help. Kate resolved to keep things
between them strictly business...until she saw the look in his eyes.
A look that matched the desire inside her....